Eliza's Dog

BETSY HEARNE

Eliza's Dog

illustrations by **ERICA THURSTON**

MARGARET K. MCELDERRY BOOKS

Margaret K. McElderry Books
An imprint of Simon & Schuster Children's Publishing Division
1230 Avenue of the Americas
New York, New York 10020

Book design by Michael Nelson

The text of this book is set in Bitstream Aldine 401
The illustrations were rendered in pencil

Printed in the United States of America
First Edition
10 9 8 7 6 5 4 3 2 1

Library of Congress Cataloging-in-Publication Data
Hearne, Betsy Gould.
Eliza's dog / Betsy Hearne; illustrated by Erica Thurston.—1st ed.
p. cm.
Summary: Nine-year-old Eliza's vacation in Ireland and England is complicated when she
acquires a bouncy sheepdog named Panda.
ISBN 0-689-80704-X
[1. Dogs—Fiction. 2. Pets—Fiction. 3. Vacations—Fiction. 4. Ireland—Fiction.
5. England—Fiction.] I. Thurston, Erica, ill. II. Title.
PZ7.H3464Eli 1996
[Fic]—dc20
95-24433

For the real Elizabeth,
who plays with dogs, words, and basketballs
—B. H.

To my youngest,
Chloe
—E. J. T.

Contents

1. Puppy Patrol

The puppies were curled together in a heap, asleep and damp from the rain. Everything in Ireland was damp from the rain. Raindrops drizzled down Eliza's neck and softened the brown cardboard box where the puppies slept. There were four—one brown and white, three black and white. Eliza knew from the dog encyclopedia how to tell male from female. After untangling the puppies and checking each one, she picked up a female. Mom said females were calmer.

The farmer who was selling the puppies looked over at Eliza. "It's a fine litter," she said. "Their mother's the best sheepdog I ever had."

All the puppies were fat and fluffy, but the one Eliza held looked like a teddy bear. It had a white nose and forehead, a white ring around its neck, white paws, and a tail that curled over its back and ended in a white tip. The rest of it was a rich, soft black except for a touch of creamy tan under its ears. Eliza cuddled it close.

"How big do you think they'll grow?" she asked. Mom said small dogs did better in the city.

"Oh, the puppies' mother is medium-size, about this tall." The farmer held her hand two feet from the ground. "The father's a bit bigger, but not much."

That might be pushing it. Mom didn't like to take chances. Well, Eliza could say medium-small. *It's going to be medium-small, Mom—just the right size.*

"How much do they cost?"

"I'm charging five pounds each for them. They're good working dogs."

Five Irish pounds was only about eight dollars in American money—definitely a point in Eliza's favor. Some of the dogs she had wanted cost hundreds of dollars, and she had wanted dozens of dogs. The entire dog encyclopedia flashed through her mind like a video on fast-forward. Over the last two years she had begged for a West Highland terrier, a sheltie, a golden retriever, a collie, a cocker spaniel, and a bichon frise.

"A bichon frise!" said her mother. "What on earth is a bichon frise?"

"Sweetpea is a bichon frise."

"Sweetpea?"

"Susie's dog. You have to come see it."

The next time Eliza's mother picked her up at Susie's apartment, Eliza introduced her to the tiny, white, perfumed bichon frise. "Isn't it adorable?" Eliza asked her mother. Her mother admired it politely. After they left, her mother said bichon frises looked yappy and smelled like bubble bath. "You want a dog, not a toy," said her mother.

"Yap, yap, yap," said Eliza.

"What did you say, Eliza?"

"Nothing, Mom."

"That sounded very rude to me," said her mother.

In the rainy town square, the little sheepdog nestled in Eliza's arms. It definitely did not smell like bubble bath.

"I call that one Panda," said the farmer. "The littlest puppy is timid, and the biggest one is bold. Panda's a good mix. She's calm, but she's lively, too. Look in her mouth. They say the best sheepdogs have blue-black coloring on the roof of their mouth. And she's got the right markings. Too much white and you can't tell them apart from the sheep. Too much black and they scare the sheep. With black and white, you can see them day or night."

Panda. Panda was a good name. Over the puppy's floppy ears, Eliza saw her mother making her way through the crowded street. Even from a distance, Mom looked mad. Eliza rubbed the wart on her thumb. She wished it would go away. Eliza's mother had no warts.

Mom squeezed her way across the square. On market day, everyone from miles around came to buy and sell their wares. Some sold carrots, some sold home-knit sweaters. Only one sold sheepdogs. Eliza wished a good mood would descend on Mom like the gentle rain.

"Eliza, where have you been?" said her mother. "We've looked everywhere. You can't just disappear without telling us where you're going. What is THAT?"

"It's a puppy, Mom."

"Eliza."

"Come on, Mom, just look at it." Eliza brought the puppy close. Her mother was nearsighted and very prejudiced against dogs. "Come on, Mom, you have to admit she's cute."

"All right, Eliza, she's cute."

Eliza knew, when she heard her mother admit to cute, that begging might pay off. Her mother hated the word "cute." She must be carried away. Eliza chose her own words carefully. Begging was an art that required patience.

Step number one was always the most important toward getting what you wanted. Without step number one, you couldn't take step number two. Eliza had been stuck on step number one for years, but she never gave up on getting a dog.

"It's a female, Mom. She's a Border collie, from a working sheepdog. She's calm but lively and she's medium-small and she's got just the right markings and she's got blue on the roof of her mouth, which is the best kind, and she costs five pounds, which is only eight dollars."

"Wait a minute, Eliza; we're just here for the summer!"

"We could take her home."

"How? Chicago is across the ocean seven thousand miles away. I don't even know if you can take animals into the U.S. from Ireland. There are all kinds of quarantine laws."

"Can't we ask?"

"I don't think it would work out. I'll talk it over with your father."

Step number two.

"Mom, you always say that. Where is he?"

"In the grocery shop. He's making baked chicken tonight."

"Mom, did you forget I'm a vegetarian? Chickens and dogs are probably related, way back through the dinosaurs. You wouldn't eat dog meat, would you? Can I stay here awhile and look at the puppies?"

Mom rolled her eyes, which Eliza hated, and turned to the farmer and said, "Hi. I'm Sarah Daly."

"I'm Meg O'Sullivan," said the farmer. "Your daughter seems to like puppies. She's welcome to stay. In fact, you're welcome to visit the farm. We've got horses, goats, sheep, cows, chickens, ducks, children—all kinds of animals. My husband stayed home today because our mare is foaling."

"How old are the children?" asked Eliza.

"They're babies, not old enough for you to play with yet, I'm afraid. But you could meet Panda's mother and grandmother. And the guinea fowl from Africa."

"Wow! A guinea fowl?" said Eliza.

"We used to have a whole flock. They're supposed to be delicious, but we never got a taste. The fox ate them first. He must not have realized they were related way back through the dinosaurs. We're hoping the last guinea fowl will hatch her eggs. There's a peacock, too."

"We'd love to come out sometime," said Mom, "but we'll have to discuss the puppy and let you know."

"Oh, Mom, can't we take it now? Somebody else

might want this one. You said we could think about a dog after my tenth birthday, and that's only a few months away. We could use the vacation to house-train the puppy. It will be a lot easier than waiting till I'm in school again and you and Dad go back to work."

"That's a point, Eliza. But we'd still have to find out about quarantines and shots and air travel."

"Actually, there's no quarantine from Ireland to the U.S.," said Meg. "It's only coming into Ireland and England that an animal has to be kept six months for rabies quarantine. We've had to check up on the laws because of our farm stock."

"How old are the puppies?" asked Mom.

Eliza held her breath. This sounded like step number three. Mom was investigating further. It was a sign of weakness.

"They're eight weeks old. The mother weaned them early. It was shearing season, and she was working hard."

"That's just the right age, Mom. The dog encyclopedia says so."

"The dog encyclopedia doesn't say anything about how to get this puppy home."

"I know a good vet, if you'd want to inquire about shots," said Meg.

"Here's your father, Eliza; thank goodness," said Mom.

Dad struggled into view with the groceries, turning sideways to get between two baby buggies on the narrow sidewalk. When he saw Eliza with the puppy, he raised one eyebrow at Eliza's mother. Eliza was familiar with that look. It meant "What's up?" and "Do you see what I see?" and "I know you see what I'm seeing—what do you think about it?" This was a promising sign. Her parents had another look that meant, "Oh no, not again." Reading signs was crucial to begging.

Eliza glanced at Meg and saw that she was staring at Mom and Dad. Eliza knew this look too—the surprise of seeing a six-foot-tall woman married to a five-foot-six-inch man. Mom, Dad, and Eliza made a staircase with a puppy at the bottom. Panda whimpered in her sleep and buried her nose in Eliza's armpit.

"Dad, can I keep her? She's a female. From a string of working sheepdogs. She's calm but lively and only costs five pounds—that's eight dollars—and she's going to be medium-small and she's got the just the right markings and she's got blue on the roof of her mouth, which is the best kind, and she's just the right age and there's no quarantine going into the United States and Meg O'Sullivan knows a good vet for shots. Mrs. O'Sullivan, this is my father, Patrick Daly. Dad, this is Meg O'Sullivan. She has a farm and we're invited out to see Panda's mother and grandmother. The dog encyclopedia says it's important to see a puppy's parents. This is Panda."

Eliza stopped talking. It was important to know when to stop talking. Dad was always happy in Ireland, and he might say yes. She really needed his vote. While it was true that Eliza had plenty of practice begging for a dog, Mom also had plenty of practice saying no. She and Mom were exactly even. Two years of begging—two years of saying no. Dad looked at the puppies for a long time. Mom looked at Dad.

"Please, Dad," begged Eliza. "Somebody else might take her if we wait. Please, please, please, please, please, please, please, please, please, please, please, please, plea—"

"That's enough, Eliza," said Mom. "You're giving me a headache."

Eliza knew she should keep quiet now. It was hard. She had to do something to help her not talk. She tried to think of words that rhymed with "please." All she could think of was fleas. *Please fleas.* Nope, wrong concept. She went through the whole alphabet. Bees? Cheese? Freeze? Jeez? *Jeez, Dad, please!* Maybe. Keys? Knees? Pees? Wrong again. Sees? Sneeze? Tease? *Please don't tease.* Would he ever make up his mind? *Please please please,* she begged silently. Could Dad be directed by mental telepathy?

Dad rubbed his finger along Panda's nose. "They're great dogs," Dad said to Mom. Then he turned to Meg. "Perhaps we could pay you to hold her for us on condition that the airline would let her on board."

"What about our week in London, Patrick?" said Mom.

"Well, we might be able to manage that. It's the long flight home afterward that I'd really worry about."

"I'll tell you what," said Meg. "You can take her with you now. If you find out right away that the transport is impossible, we'll take her back. We're not going to be able to sell all the puppies today anyway because of the rain. One woman has spoken for the male, and I'll bring the others back to the square next Friday. It's time for us to be getting home."

"Oh, thank you, thank you, thank you, thank you, thank—"

"All right, Eliza, that's enough," said Mom. "Calm down."

Thank you, spank you, Eliza said to herself.

"What should I feed her?" she asked out loud.

"Oh, any kind of dog food. We boil up bones for them on the farm. That's all we have. She'll be hungry. We didn't feed the pups much this morning because we were afraid they would throw up on the ride into town."

Mom rolled her eyes at Dad. Eliza hugged Panda closer. Panda yelped.

"Okay," said Dad. "I'll go back and buy the dog food. Eliza, you'd better get Panda into the car before she turns into soup."

Rain had flattened the puppy's thick fur, but when Eliza settled into the backseat, Panda made a warm nest in her lap. Finally, Eliza had some company in the backseat. She would have company from now on, day in and day out, and never ever be all by herself again. Ever, ever, ever, amen.

As they started along the steep rocky road toward the cottage they had rented, Dad sang out, "Cow patrol!" A herd of black-and-white holstein cows filled the road ahead, jostling each other to get away from the black-and-white sheepdog that darted at their heels. The cows seemed about to stampede the car, but Eliza didn't panic. The cows panicked. With their eyes rolling and their udders swinging, they stopped and stared as if the car held a pack of wolves. Every afternoon, the farmer moved his herd from a nearby field to his barn for milking. Every afternoon, the cows blocked the road. Every afternoon they acted as if every car they met was a pack of wolves. The only thing to do was sit still and wait. You couldn't rush a cow. The animals finally divided around the car like a black-and-white river, mooing and swishing their tails. They left a trail of cow poop behind them.

"Yuck," said Eliza as Dad waved to the farmer and started driving over the splats of dung.

"You'll be cleaning up after Panda soon enough," said Mom. "Remember the deal."

Eliza nodded her head. *Fuss, fuss. Fuss, cuss.* Of course she would clean up. She still couldn't believe it was real, this puppy that was curled up in her arms. *A real deal, never a squeal.* Eliza rhymed in time to the curves as the car rolled along the rocky coast of Bantry Bay.

Dad said silly rhymes were called doggerel and doggerel was pretty low on the totem pole of literature, but personally Eliza liked doggerel. Just the sound of it. Doggerel had a GRRRRRRRR sound, like Lassie about to leap. *Panda the doggerel dog. How do you feel? Want a meal? How about veal? Stay at my heel. See that seal?* Eliza bounced Panda a bit with each rhyme. She strained to see if there really were any seals bobbing among the rocks below, where they often swam.

Dad was doing his roller-coaster act on the road, and the car swung up and over the hills in a way that Eliza found thrilling. Her stomach and heart seemed to change places.

"Castle patrol," Dad called as they passed a huge stone tower with crumbling walls. He slowed down for a good look at the landmark they loved.

"We're almost home," Eliza crooned to Panda as they picked up speed again. "Do you think she's okay, Mom? She's so quiet. She's hardly moved since we got in the car."

With her fur dry again, Panda looked like a stuffed toy with a heartbeat.

"She couldn't wiggle if she wanted to, Eliza. You're squeezing her."

"I'm not squeezing her, Mom. The dog encyclopedia says that puppies need to feel loved."

Panda's soft, dark eyes opened wide, and she began licking Eliza's hand with a tiny pink tongue. "Look, Mom, see how much she loves me?"

Panda opened her mouth a little wider and threw up all over Eliza's lap.

"Oh, gross. Dad, stop the car. Mom, HELP!" Eliza wailed.

"Puppy patrol," shouted Dad as he swerved the car to the side of the road. Mom grabbed the ever-ready roll of paper towels.

"Here, Eliza; to love a dog is to clean up after it," said Mom.

"But she threw up," Eliza wailed.

"The pup threw up! It rhymes," said Dad.

From the middle of the mess, Panda pushed a wet black nose against Eliza's neck. She was real.

2. Designer Dog

Late in the afternoon, Dad finally hung up the phone. Eliza hung on every word. "Okay, here's the deal," he said. "The airline says we can take Panda as excess baggage if she fits into a sixteen-inch by twenty-one–inch box no more than eight inches high, so it will go under the seat. We can't count on a pressurized baggage compartment on our flight over to London or back to Chicago, either. So if the baggage compartment isn't pressurized, and she doesn't fit into the box under the seat, we're out of luck."

Eliza rubbed the wart on her thumb.

"Eliza," said Mom, "you need to think about this

carefully. It's not too late to return Panda. I know you've wanted a dog for a long time, and Panda is ideal in some ways. But taking her home is going to change our trip. You'll have to start house-training her here. Then you'll have to start over with a new routine when we get home. Also, we may not be able to see the sights we wanted to in London."

"Can we still go to the Tower and Madame Tussaud's Wax Museum?"

"I can't promise you that. We'll just have to wait and see. We don't even know if the hotel that we've booked will accept dogs, or if dogs can go on buses and trains."

"She's so little—no one will even notice her."

"That's another thing. If she grows bigger than the carrying case—and the carrying case will be hard to track down without making a two-hour trip to the city—Cork is the closest—we'll have to find a home for her here."

"I want her, Mom. No matter what. Even if I can't see all the stuff in London."

"I don't know, Eliza."

"I do, Mom; I really do. She has to go home with us."

"Then she has to stay small."

Eliza lifted one of Panda's furry ears. "G-r-o-w s-l-o-w-l-y," she whispered.

Panda struggled to get down. In spite of what the dog

encyclopedia said about being loved, she did not seem to love being heaved up and down in Eliza's arms like an elevator. She did not seem to care for someone breathing in her ear, either. Panda shook her head and snapped at the air. The furry ear Eliza was whispering into flopped inside out.

"Hey, with her ear flipped, she looks like a werewolf. C'mon, Panda, it's stopped raining. Let's go swing."

"Don't swing too hard. Remember, she just wolfed down a dog biscuit," said Mom.

"Okay, Panda, I'll swing. You can practice not throwing up."

Panda tumbled after Eliza, rolling halfway down the grassy hill like a furry black-and-white soccer ball. Dad had rigged up a swing with heavy nylon rope tied around a tree branch. He was going to make it a Tarzan vine, but they had found a thick board down by the beach, worn smooth by the sea, with two holes just right for the rope. The holes had rust stains around them, probably from screws that had fastened the board to part of a boat. Maybe a wrecked boat. Eliza had once considered begging for a Newfoundland in case she was ever shipwrecked. A shipwreck, as Eliza imagined it, might not be so bad. *The Newfoundland retrieved her, swimming through the stormy waves, then plunged back for Mom and Dad, bringing them each to shore. They were forever grateful, allowing Eliza to keep all of the Newfoundland puppies born to that brave dog shortly after the rescue.*

After 999 dream dogs, it was hard to believe she had a real one. Eliza backed the swing up to the top of the hill and sailed out as if her feet would touch the sun, which had just popped through the clouds. The summer sun stayed up late in Ireland, and so did everybody else. The bay sparkled below. A fishing boat chugged past, with gulls riding the wind behind it. The donkeys in the next field—Maggie, Geraldine, and Geraldine's shaggy white foal, Gertrude—grazed near a clump of wildflowers.

Panda ran back and forth under the swing, chasing the piece of rope that dragged from the knot underneath. Sometimes she got mixed up and chased her tail instead. Finally she flopped under the bushes, where Eliza had made a hideout. Eliza crawled in under the damp, arching branches, and Panda rolled over for a stomach rub. Her round stomach had a beautiful pattern of black and white.

"You're a Designer Dog, Panda, just like my Designer Jeans. See? The Dog with a Difference."

Panda began licking the ankle of Eliza's new jeans. Eliza had begged for designer jeans for an entire year. She had used steps one through ten, including a survey of all her friends who had designer jeans. The all-my-friends argument never worked. Mom had said, "Designer jeans are too expensive, Eliza, and they're just a trend. If you still want them next year, we'll see." Eliza had not given up. Next year came, and she still wanted designer jeans, and she finally, at long last, got them. These were the only pair she would ever get, Mom said.

Till I'm grown up and can pay for them myself, Eliza had argued silently as they left the designer jeans store. She did not argue out loud in case Mom got mad and took back the designer jeans to teach her a lesson. Mom did not always understand the difference between arguing and sassing. Sassing was a sin in the Daly family.

Panda began chewing on the hem of the designer jeans, and Eliza pulled her leg away. Panda bit down harder and pulled back.

"Ow! Stop that. Stop it!" The more Eliza pulled, the harder Panda chomped down with her needle-sharp teeth. Eliza jumped up and tried to run. Panda held on, gargling puppy growls from the back of her throat and hanging on to Eliza's leg like a werewolf mangling its victim.

"Dad," she screamed, "she won't let go!" Dad and Mom both ran out of the house. As soon as Dad grabbed Panda, she let go and started chewing on his fingers.

"She bites!" cried Eliza.

"No, honey, she just chews. She thinks you're another puppy. That's the way they play with each other—nip and tackle. We have to get chewing toys for her. Watch."

Dad picked up a piece of rope left over from making the swing and knotted it in three places. Then he dragged it in front of Panda's nose. Panda pounced on the rope and tackled it with her teeth.

ROOF! ROOF! Her puppy barks sounded like the Chipmunks on Saturday-morning cartoons.

"Rope! Rope!" yelled Dad, running back and forth across the grass.

ROOF!

"Rope!"

Panda shook the rope as if it were a rat. When she stopped, it hung limp from her mouth, with both ends unraveled.

"Dead rope," said Dad. "She must be part terrier, the way she hangs on. Just like Eliza."

"Dad."

"I'd better start calling the vet and the hotel and the pet shop, if there is one."

"Let's go down to the shore before it gets dark, Eliza," said Mom. "Bring that string from the kitchen. We'll have to braid Panda a collar and use my old belt for a leash until we get a real one."

When they finished, Eliza knotted the collar braid loosely around Panda's neck and slipped the belt through it. "Come on, Panda, let's go for a walk."

Panda sat down.

"Start walking, Eliza; she'll follow you," said Mom. "That's what sheepdogs are famous for. They'll herd anything, even people. It may be a problem for us back in the city."

Sure enough, as long as Eliza walked a little ahead, Panda trotted behind. When they reached the shore, Panda had a hard time keeping up. The rocks were bigger than she was. Eliza scooped her up, and Mom speeded up.

"Slow down, Mom," Eliza called. Carrying Panda made it awkward to jump from rock to rock.

"I need to stretch my legs, Eliza. I'll meet you by the big tidal pool."

Mom took off like a streak over and around the rocks. Eliza sighed. Mom claimed she had to run so that she could keep up with her track and basketball teams. She coached at the same university where Dad taught history, but there was a big difference. Coaches were a lot bossier than history teachers. Plus, coaching meant a lot of night games away, so during the school year Mom was either at home and bossy, or gone. Every time Mom went out of town, she reminded Eliza of how lucky they were to have summers off together. Then she left.

"But now I have you to keep me company, Panda," huffed Eliza as her mother disappeared around a curve in the shore. "You wouldn't leave me behind, would you? Not like some people we know—Mom, for instance. Or Mary."

Eliza had a wonderful half sister, Mary. Eliza knew Mary was wonderful because everyone said so. Wonderful Mary went to college and was too grown-up to play when she came home for visits, which wasn't often because she got summer jobs away from home. What good was a sister who's never home? And when she did come home, Mary had long dinners and boring conversations with Mom and Dad, even though Eliza tried to introduce interesting topics such as getting a dog. But no, they'd rather pay attention to what Eliza did wrong. *Eliza felt surrounded by a posse of bossy voices:* "Don't interrupt again, Eliza." "Don't reach across the table, Eliza." "Nice manners, twerp!" Someday, she would strike back. "Don't interrupt!" she would shout at Mom. "Don't reach across the table," she'd order Dad. "Nice manners, twerp!" she'd tell Mary with withering scorn.

If Mary wasn't talking to her parents about boring subjects, she was reading boring books. Mary did not watch TV or beg to rent movies for the VCR. Mary had long legs and often ran track with Mom. Mary did not have warts. Eliza smoothed the fur on Panda's nose.

Panda did not seem to mind the wart on Eliza's thumb. Panda did not say, "Gross wart, Eliza!" Eliza shifted the puppy to one arm and picked up a round, flat stone with the other. Taking careful aim, she threw it in a curve across the water. Three skips. Not bad.

Mom was leaning over one of the tidal pools when Eliza and Panda caught up. Some of the biggest rocks had cracks and holes that served as deep dishes for seawater. When the tide came in, the dishes filled up, and when the tide went out, Eliza could search the pools that remained for crabs, sea urchins, and odd-shaped tiny fish that hid under bits of seaweed. She put Panda down and knelt beside her mother.

"Look, Eliza, between those two rocks."

"Oh, Mom, an orange starfish. I've never seen such a big one." The starfish seemed to slide along the rock, but it was really moved along by hundreds of tiny white tentacles under its body.

"Can we take this one home, Mom, please?"

"No, Eliza, that's not fair. Let's watch it in the pool."

"Just while we're here. I could make a sea tank in the dishpan."

"You can't make a real copy of its home. You'd have to change the water every six hours, just like the tides, and blow on it like wind that moves the water. You'd have to catch clams and mussels, and still it might not eat them."

"I could try."

"Eliza, it took thousands of years for tide-pool creatures to adapt so perfectly to their environment. They'd die in a dishpan after a few days. You have to respect their nature."

"I know that, Mom. But anyway, the fishermen say they're a natural nuisance. Starfish eat shellfish, so the fishermen can't get as many. And starfish are hard to get rid of. They regenerate even if you chop them up."

"Eliza, you're not going to argue me into choosing starfish or fishermen. I'm not taking sides, and you're not taking any starfish home."

"Oh, Mom."

Eliza knew from experience that she would lose this argument. She could smell a lost argument a mile away. She could almost taste it. Panda shoved next to her, lapped at the water, and leaped back.

"Too salty, Panda? We'll get you some water back home. And food. You can try out your new Puppy Chow. Wow, chow!"

"We'd better get back and help Dad start dinner too, Eliza. It looks like a storm's coming. Mr. Minehan in the shop said there was going to be another drop of rain tonight. That means a downpour."

As Eliza and her mother walked back up the lane, clouds covered the sun. The bay grew choppy. Near the cottage, Panda sniffed at a tree and suddenly squatted down.

"Hey, Mom, she's peeing."

"What a talented dog!"

"No, really, maybe she's just naturally house-trained. Good dog! Good dog!" Panda wiggled around Eliza's feet in circles, dancing with Eliza's delight.

"Oh, Mom, it's so much fun to have a dog."

"We'll see," said Mom. "Sometimes it is and sometimes it isn't."

As soon as they got home, Eliza poured a little warm milk over the dry dog food. Panda dove into the milk, lapping it up greedily and crunching the brown nuggets.

"I wonder what they taste like," said Eliza. She reached into the bag and nibbled on a piece. "Nothing. They taste like nothing, Panda. You deserve better."

"She deserves to go out again, after all that food, Eliza. Look at her stomach."

Eliza took the bulging puppy out into the yard, but Panda just lay down at Eliza's feet and closed her eyes.

"Okay, Panda, we'll try again later." Panda shadowed Eliza back into the kitchen.

"Did she go?" asked Mom.

"Too tired," said Eliza.

"You'd better take her out again soon."

"I know, Mom."

"She's your responsibility."

"I know, Mom."

"You won't forget?"

"MOM!"

"All right. Dad wants to start a fire."

As darkness fell, along with a lot of rain, Eliza helped her father lay a fire in the huge old fireplace. First the crumpled newspaper, then the twigs, then the sticks in a teepee shape over the paper and twigs, then the peat bricks circling the teepee. When the fire was glowing, she went into the bathroom to wash up for dinner. Panda trotted along behind her. The toilet was old-fashioned, with a sign printed on it: DO NOT THROW FOREIGN BODIES IN THE W.C. BOWL (OTHERWISE THEY MAY CLOG THE DRAINPIPE).

"See that, Panda? No foreign bodies in the toilet. That includes you. You're safe." Panda sniffed at the bath mat, waved her curly tail, hunched her back end, and did a poop beside the bathtub.

"No, Panda, no! Bad dog!"

Mom appeared in the doorway. Silently she handed Eliza paper towels and a bottle of white vinegar, which

Dad had bought with the dog food. What went in would come out, he said, and white vinegar was good for deodorizing puppy odors.

"Dinner's ready, when you finish cleaning up," said Mom.

"Yuck. I'm not very hungry now."

But when they all sat down and Mom lit the candles, the smell of Dad's baked chicken with gravy and brown rice made Eliza's stomach growl. Tomorrow she would be a vegetarian.

Just as she took her first bite, there was a crunching sound from under the table.

"Eliza, is that you?" Dad said. Eliza swallowed, but the crunching sound continued.

"It's Panda," said Mom. "I gave her last night's beef bone to work on instead of my shoe."

Mom was very particular about her running shoes. Personally, Eliza did not mind a few tooth marks on her sneakers.

For a while everybody chewed together, but Mom and Dad chewed very slowly. Eliza ate in record time and was finished long before her parents, who were discussing important subjects again. They ate so slowly that sometimes Eliza wanted to scream.

The crunching grew louder. Eliza leaned sideways

and looked under the table. "Nice manners, twerp!"

"What did you say, Eliza?"

"I was talking to Panda. May I please be excused?" she asked.

"Only if you take the source of that bone-crunching sound with you. And take out your dishes, too," said Dad.

"And don't forget to take the puppy out if you see her sniffing around," added Mom.

Eliza went into the living room and added several pieces of peat to the fire. It was cozy, with the rain beating down outside and the waves pounding the shore below. She pulled up a chair to the table they had set up for rainy-day work. There were a lot of rainy days in Ireland. Without sisters or brothers or friends around, a person had to be expert at entertaining herself. Eliza's current project was rock painting. She had found the idea in a tourist shop where painted rocks cost a pound each—a dollar and seventy-five cents! "You can paint your own," Dad had said, and had bought her a set of oil paints that cost only a pound. For less than the cost of one tourist-shop rock, she had already painted ten rocks, and the tubes of paint were not even half empty yet. Eliza finished the rock she was working on, a design of circles in red and yellow. Then she started one in triangles of blue and green, with wiggly lines. She looked up from her second triangle to see Panda sniffing at the edge of the rug.

"Okay, Panda. I'll take you out as soon as I finish this green."

Panda squatted and squirted the rug.

Eliza jumped up and yelled, "Bad dog, Panda. BAD DOG!" She took the puppy into the backyard. The rain had slowed to a gusty sprinkle, but the wind was high. Eliza looked up at the moon, fading in and out of a black-and-silver cloud that sent showers spraying down. The black-and-silver cloud threw up some wind. Then it chewed on the moon. Then it peed rain. Then it pooped out a little pile of clouds. The black-and-silver cloud looked a lot like a dog, and it was growing.

3. Dog Tired

The dog cloud turned into a werewolf cloud, which thinned to a wispy ghost while Eliza walked around the yard and Panda explored the bushes. The night was quiet as a tomb. No cars or trucks traveled the lonely road to the sea. No airplanes flew overhead. The loudest sound came from the donkeys cropping grass beside the fence. Crunch, crunch, crunch. Then the cropping stopped, and the quiet covered her like moonlight. "The moon was a ghostly galleon tossed upon cloudy seas," her father would say when he saw the moon. Eliza began to think about ghostly galleons and about the poem her father always quoted. "The road was a ribbon of moonlight over the purple moor." There was a graveyard up the road, and the ghosts were probably lonely for human company right now. "And the highwayman came riding—riding—riding. . . ." The more Eliza thought about it, the more likely it seemed that a ghost might come visiting any minute. A streak of white zoomed beside her and she jumped and the streak of white crunched her shoe. Panda was herding her feet.

"Stop it!" Eliza shrieked.

No one heard her. The wind-twisted trees threw shadows across the lawn. "The wind was a torrent of darkness among the gusty trees." Sometimes when Eliza couldn't sleep, Dad said the whole poem about the highwayman who rode the night road toward his true love, named Bess. "I'll come to thee by moonlight. . . ." Something could come to Eliza by moonlight. She shivered. It was definitely time to go inside. It was time to make some noise. Chicago was never this quiet. Chicago seemed not just seven thousand miles away, but seven thousand years away. *She was a young traveler lost in the dark trees and stormy seas and ghostly silence, calling on her dog to find the way home.* Eliza reached down and stroked Panda, damp from the rain-soaked grass.

"Come on, this is the magic moment we've all been

waiting for. Squirt the dirt, twerp." And Panda did.

"Good dog. GREAT DOG, Miss Piss!" *Don't be crude, Eliza.*

Back inside the house, Eliza detoured to the kitchen for the white vinegar to clean the living-room rug where Panda had peed.

"Having an after-dinner drink?" asked Dad.

"It wasn't her fault, Dad. I didn't put her out in time."

"Eliza," said Mom.

"I'm sorry."

"Sorry is too late."

"Well, you and Panda both need to get used to things," said Dad. "Mom and I will come in by the fire as soon as we finish up here."

Irish music sang from the tape player. *Fiddley-diddley.* No rock music, of course. Mom and Dad came here for peace and quiet. *Fiddley-diddley-piddley.* And no television in the cottage. Their house sitter back home had promised to tape Eliza's favorite shows. Meanwhile, there was solitaire, and sometimes her parents would play casino or gin if she asked them in just the right way, at just the right time—after dinner but before they got too tired.

A card game wasn't as good as TV, but at least they played cards together. Back home they never watched TV together. Dad did not appreciate MTV, and Eliza did not appreciate the news, which should be called the "olds" because every channel kept saying and showing the same old stuff every hour on the hour, which was boring even if the news was not boring to begin with, which it usually was. Sitcoms made Mom roll her eyes. Talk shows were okay, but her parents said they'd rather talk to each other. Of course, that left Eliza out, because everything they talked about was boring. They never argued like people did on talk shows. It was fun to argue, and it was fun to watch other people argue. Even when talk shows got boring, they were nice and noisy. Personally, Eliza preferred to hear people interrupting each other in loud, excited voices than to be all alone with nobody to talk to but herself. She had actually considered becoming a talk-show hostess.

"Dahling, you look wonderful tonight. Tell us about your new movie!" Or maybe she would be the famous person being interviewed: *"Yes, I have trained many sheepdogs, and they've all won blue ribbons!"* She could put on a TV show now for her parents, a talk show they'd love. Eliza added more peat to the fire, lined up her best rocks, cleared the table by dumping the rest of the craft stuff in her room, and began to plan her show. She didn't have much time. Mom and Dad must be almost done in the kitchen. Panda rolled over beside her and twitched.

"You're going to be the star of the show, Panda."

Dad came and sat in the big chair. "That's a good fire you've got going there, honey."

Mom squeezed in beside him. "And the nice fresh smell of vinegar!"

"I said I was sorry, Mom. Okay, you guys. No casino tonight. I'm going to do a TV show for you." Eliza set Panda on a pillow on one side of the table, where the puppy plumped down with a sigh. Eliza stood by the other side of the table.

"Ladies and gentlemen," she said, "we have with us tonight a charming guest, well known to many as Ms. PANDA!"

Mom and Dad clapped politely. Panda raised her head at the sound.

"Ms. Panda, tell us what's the hardest thing about being a puppy?"

Eliza raced to the other end of the table and spoke in a high, fast, Chipmunk voice. "Knowing where to go to the bathroom."

Eliza moved back to her own side of the table. "Do you have any other special worries?"

"That I'll grow up to be a big, ugly dog," squeaked Eliza from Panda's end of the table.

"Ms. Panda, with that black-and-white coat, you look like a designer dog! I'm sure you're going to be gorgeous and MEDIUM-SMALL—just the right size for a city dog. And, while you grow, we're going to talk to our next guest, MR. ROCK!"

Mom and Dad clapped again.

"Mr. Rock, how does it feel to be granite?"

"Heavy. Very, very, very, very, very, very, very, very heavy," said Eliza in a deep voice.

"What's the hardest thing about being a rock?"

"People drop you. Like this, THUMP. They can't squash you, but they do drop you. DUMP THUMP BUMP LUMP."

"You sound like a rock concert!"

"I am stoned."

"Eliza Daly!" Mom interrupted.

"Mom, you can't talk to a television set. It can say anything it wants. And speaking of art, Mr. Rock, if you were to be painted, what design would you choose?"

"Circles. Triangles. Popsicles. Flowers. Maybe a puppy."

"Well, Ms. Panda, what do you think of that? Everybody loves a puppy. Folks, we're going to be joined by a new guest right after these commercials."

Eliza picked up the bottle of white vinegar and pretended to pour it into her orange-juice glass. Then, with a flourish, she picked up the glass and drained it with loud glug-glug sounds. "Mmmm," she said, wiping her mouth with her sleeve. "Worth waiting for!"

Then she leaped up from the table and pointed to the grass stains spread over her shirt. "See this dirt and grime?"

She grabbed the paint-tube box. "See this box of laundry soap?"

She twirled to face the wall, whipped off her shirt, and put it on inside out. Then she turned again and spread her arms wide. "Nothing washes like soap."

The audience cheered.

"Not for the commercials," Eliza hissed at her parents.

"And now, ladies and gentlemen, our last guest, MR. CARD!"

Her parents clapped quietly.

"Mr. Card, how does it feel to be a ten of hearts?"

"Flat," said Eliza in a thin voice.

"What's the hardest thing about being a card?"

"Getting shuffled around like this."

"Oh, I'm sorry, Mr. Card."

"That's all right; people do it all the time. I don't mind so much when I'm playing."

"Mr. Card, you have a handsome design on your back."

"I never look back."

"I guess that would be cheating. Well, Mr. Card, you're a real trump, but it looks as though we've run out of time. I'll just stack you back with your friends here.

And now, ladies and gentlemen, stay tuned for another boring broadcast of the news. Ta-da!"

Mom and Dad both applauded.

"I wish the real shows were as imaginative as you are, Eliza," said Dad.

"I wish you didn't watch so many of them," said Mom.

"I have to watch them, Mom, or I wouldn't know about them, and then I couldn't imagine them."

"Well, I'm too tired to argue about TV tonight. Better get that puppy out one more time."

Dad helped take Panda for a bedtime sniff around the yard. "'The moon was a ghostly galleon tossed upon cloudy seas,'" said Dad, looking up at the sky.

"I know, Dad, and 'the road was a ribbon of moonlight.'" Eliza looked up the road, but with Dad around, no ghosts came near. She hopscotched over small shadows across the lawn while Panda chased her feet, and afterward she hopscotched over the playing cards, rocks, and paint jars that she had dumped on the floor of her room after cleaning off the craft table. Then Eliza did her flying leap into bed, with Panda bouncing up beside her. Mom read aloud two more chapters of *Mine for Keeps,* which had a lot of good advice about training dogs, and turned out the light and kissed Eliza good night.

"And now," said Mom, "tell the audience, what's the hardest thing about being Eliza?"

"That we might have to leave Panda behind. What if she grows too much to go back home with us?"

"We'll just have to hope for the best and look around for a good home, in case she does grow too much. Right now, Panda's going to the kitchen." Mom lifted the puppy up from her nest in Eliza's blankets.

"No, Mom, let her sleep here!"

"Eliza, your room would smell like a barnyard by morning. We're lucky we can close her up in the kitchen here. Back home, with no door between the kitchen and living room, Panda's going to sleep in the basement until she's completely house-trained."

"But she'll be lonely all by herself in the dark."

"She'll be lonely for a little while and then she'll settle down. Believe me, better a lonely puppy than a grouchy mother. This is my vacation too, you know."

"Oh, fine! But Mom, you know Lady and the Tramp? How come they never went to the bathroom, even on walks?"

"That's the difference between movies and life, Eliza."

"Well, I like Panda even if she does pee and poop and throw up."

"We're counting on that, Eliza Lou. Now go to sleep."

Panda yelped for five minutes. Personally, Eliza could sympathize with yelping for help in a dark, lonely room. Dogs and children should be allowed to stay up as late as they wanted and should not be shut up in different rooms. *The proud, house-trained, medium-small Border collie trotted by her side into the living room, turned on the TV with its nose, and curled up beside her with a loving glance. When their favorite show came on, Eliza shared a huge bowl of buttered popcorn with her dog. The proud, house-trained, medium-small Border collie never begged, but licked each kernel from her hand carefully so that its smooth white teeth would not accidentally wolf down her fingers instead of the popcorn.*

Finally the yelping in the kitchen stopped. The house grew quiet except for the soft murmur of Mom and Dad getting into bed, and Eliza whispering to her pillow, "Don't grow, Panda; please don't grow."

The pillow did not answer.

4. Doggone

Panda was growing.

Eliza cut the cheese into three cubes. Panda sniffed the air and drooled—she knew what was coming. Eliza marched from the kitchen to the living room as Panda jumped and nipped at her legs, herding her toward the box.

"Stop it, Panda. Now sit."

Panda sat. Eliza gave her one cube of cheese.

"Box, Panda, box." Eliza threw another piece of cheese into the box. The puppy dove in after it. As Panda gobbled up the cheese, Eliza closed the wire door. When Panda turned around, she was neatly locked in the box.

"Good dog," said Eliza. "Now say, 'cheese please.'" Panda did not say anything, but Eliza slipped the last piece of cheese through the grate anyway, and Panda snapped it up.

Every day, Eliza and Panda practiced box. Every day Panda stayed inside a little longer, getting used to the tiny, closed space. Every day, the box was a tighter fit. Panda was not growing slowly. When she went into the box, her tail stuck out, and it was getting harder for her to turn around. If she turned around, her nose stuck out. She was comfortable lying down but crowded standing up.

Every time Panda went into the box, Eliza's stomach got tighter. She wanted the time to hurry by so that Panda wouldn't grow too much, but she also wanted their vacation to last as long as possible in case Panda did grow too much. What if they had to leave Panda in Ireland? Eliza rubbed the wart on her thumb. Panda turned around in the box and waited for another piece of cheese.

"Doggone it, Panda, stop growing." "Doggone" was as close to swearing as Eliza was allowed. Maybe if she said it a lot, "doggone" would happen. *Dog going, dog going, dog gone*—all the way from Ireland to Chicago.

"Patrick, have you called the hotel about the puppy yet?" asked Mom.

"I'm afraid they'll say no," said Dad. "What if we just

show up with the puppy and throw ourselves on their mercy?"

"That's taking a big risk. What if they say no when we get there and we can't find another place to stay?"

"Oh, we'll work out something," said Dad.

Eliza picked on her wart. Would it ever come off? Did you outgrow warts? Would Panda outgrow her box?

The days built up like thunderclouds. Finally the last morning broke. While Mom and Dad loaded the car, Eliza practiced box one more time. Panda still fit, barely. At least she'd make it to London. If she grew much in London, there'd be no hope. *Hope, soap.* Mom had soaped her swollen finger once after a basketball injury, to get her wedding ring off. They could soap Panda to slip her into the box. *"This is the cleanest dog ever to enter the United States," said the customs official. "But she needs rinsing."*

"Take her out to the yard one more time," said Mom. "It's going to be a long trip."

Panda trotted right behind Eliza's feet, nose to ankle, as if she knew they were going somewhere. Every time Eliza stopped, Panda sat down.

"Please, Panda; there's your favorite bush," begged Eliza.

"Maybe she won't go—she didn't have any breakfast," said Mom. "This is going to be a VERY long trip."

Eliza turned away and made her grouchy-Mom face at the bay, where no one could see her but the seagulls. Panda panted.

They all squeezed into the car, and Dad drove s-l-o-w-l-y, especially over the hills and around the curves. Most of the road was over hills and around curves. It took a long time to get to the airport, but Panda did not throw up.

When they checked their bags, Dad asked once more about boarding Panda. Eliza held her breath.

"What a sweet puppy!" said the woman at the counter. "You'll have no problem. Just put her in the box and take her through the security gate a half hour before flight time."

Eliza breathed again. They were on their way. She got a plastic bag of cheese cubes out of her pocket, and Panda dove into the box. This time the cheese was wrapped around a small yellow pill that was supposed to keep puppies quiet for three hours.

"We may have to give her several of these on the transatlantic flight," said Mom.

"She'll be a drug addict by the time we get home," Eliza complained.

"Just a cheese addict," said Dad. "She ate all our good Irish cheddar, getting used to that box." He put his bag of books and papers on the moving belt and stepped through the security gate. Mom laid her shoulder bag flat and followed him. Eliza started through the gate with the box. It wouldn't be healthy for Panda to get x-rayed. Suddenly a guard stepped up.

"Miss, no animals past this point."

Dad turned to explain. "We were told to bring her on board in a box that would fit under the seat."

"I'm sorry, sir, but dogs can't go in the cabin."

"But we phoned the airline several times. This is exactly what they told us to do. And so did the person who checked us in."

"You must have received the wrong information, sir. The dog will have to go into baggage."

"We were told the baggage compartment isn't pressurized," said Mom.

A picture of Panda, limp and depressurized, flashed across Eliza's mind before she could eject it.

"We'll have to check, ma'am. If you would just step over to that official in the red coat so the line can move on."

The official in the red coat was busy with someone else. As Mom and Dad waited to talk to him, Eliza felt tears pushing against her eyelids. They'd have to leave Panda behind. All that waiting and hoping and arguing and begging for a dog, all for nothing. All the times she had cleaned the stupid hamsters' cage at school so that the teachers would tell her parents how responsible she was with animals, all for nothing. Panda's warm, furry, black-and-white self would be taken away from her forever, all for nothing. And how would Panda feel, getting left behind? Eliza knew how she would feel. Getting left behind was the worst feeling of all. The tears began to squeeze through. All for nothing.

Dad patted her back. "Don't cry," he said.

Why not? thought Eliza. *Why not?*

Dad and Mom finally talked to the red-coated official, and then he talked and then they talked and then he talked. The airport was noisy, and Eliza couldn't follow the discussion. Flight time was getting close. The red-coated official made a phone call. Everybody looked angry but too polite to say so. The red-coated official hung up the phone, said something to Dad, and turned to the next person waiting for his attention.

"We were given the wrong information after all," Dad told Eliza. "But we're in luck. The baggage compartment is pressurized, so Panda can be stowed there in the box. Give her to the guard, Eliza, and he'll see that she's taken care of."

Everything looked blurred through Eliza's wet eyes.

Panda's eyes looked dull too, and half closed with the sedative. Eliza hugged the box, handed it over to the guard, stepped through the gate, and looked back. The guard and the puppy box were gone. After Eliza boarded with Mom and Dad, they waited for a long time. Whatever was happening, Panda must be scared. Suddenly, the engines started with a whine that rose to a violent pitch. The plane shook and vibrated down the runway. Eliza could not help imagining her puppy shivering all alone in the dark hold, a strange cold place with huge noises roaring all around— like a lion's den.

Eliza snuffled.

"She's going to be okay, Eliza," said Dad.

"Even if she is, she'll never forgive me, Dad. It's like I've thrown her to the lions or something."

"Don't overdramatize, Eliza," said Mom sharply. "You'll just make it worse." But she picked up Eliza's hand, and Dad took the other one. They held her hands, one on each side, all the way to London.

When the plane landed, they made their way through crowds of people to the baggage-claim area. Their suitcases were there, but the puppy box was nowhere in sight. Eliza's stomach did a double knot. Panda could be lost— or someone might have gotten here first and stolen her. Or she could be sick. There might not have been enough air in the baggage compartment for a puppy. Bags didn't need to breathe. Or maybe the unloaders didn't see her and left her on the plane, way back in a corner of the baggage compartment. By this time, the plane would be on its way somewhere else. Panda could end up in India, unclaimed. She could die of hunger, circling the world in the darkest corner of the baggage compartment.

Dad asked an attendant, who directed them to an information booth, where they were directed to another area, where a huge cage waited, empty.

"Looks like we're in the right place," said Dad. "Here's where they keep the lions."

"Ha-ha, Dad."

"Come on, Eliza, cheer up. They just had a lot of baggage to unload."

"Panda is not baggage, Dad. They should have unloaded her first. She's a living, breathing dog!"

"We certainly hope so, Eliza Lou."

"Patrick!" Mom rolled her eyes at him. It was satisfying to see Mom roll her eyes at somebody else for a change.

For good luck, Eliza crossed her own eyes and all of her fingers and toes while she waited. After a while, her eyes gave up. Another half hour dragged by. Finally, reflected in the smooth polished floor way down the hall, a woman appeared carrying Panda's box. Almost everyone else had left the baggage area, and her footsteps echoed with a hollow tick tock, tick tock, tick tock.

Eliza rushed up to her and peered into the box. "She's still breathing!"

"Of course she is," Dad said behind her. "I told you it would work out."

"Let's get settled in the hotel before you get too optimistic," said Mom.

"Oh, Mom," said Eliza.

They gathered everything up and walked outside to a line of big round-topped black taxis waiting to take people into the city. The ride was smooth. Panda hardly stirred.

"Can I take her out of the box?" asked Eliza.

"Better not till we get past the hotel hurdle," said Dad.

The taxi pulled up to the sidewalk near a tall stone building. While Eliza carried Panda's box, Mom and Dad grabbed the bags and led the way into a dark lobby. This didn't look much like a family motel with pet facilities. A short hotel clerk eyed them curiously.

Eliza tried to be invisible. *Look at my mother and father. My mother is a giant. My father is a midget. Feel free to stare at them. Everybody does. Do not notice my dog.*

The hotel clerk immediately noticed Eliza's dog. Panda's furry black-and-white face was pressed against the wire door at one end of the box.

"A sheepdog," he said quietly.

Eliza held her breath.

"We're not supposed to have dogs." He paused.

How long could she hold her breath?

"She's very well behaved," said Dad. "We got her in Ireland to keep our daughter company at home in the States."

"I'm Irish myself," said the hotel clerk. "You couldn't do better than a sheepdog. Just keep her quiet in the room, if you don't mind, and carry her down the stairs for walks. The manager won't toss you out once you're in."

"Bless the Irish," muttered Mom as they climbed the stairs up to their room.

"Not everyone feels that way, my dear, but fortunately you do," said Dad. He winked one of his sea-blue eyes at Eliza. "Let's go look at London."

5. First-class Dog

London, it turned out, was hot. The city was in the middle of a heat wave, with record highs in the nineties, day after day. Since London was usually cool and rainy, none of the buildings were air-conditioned. The rooms felt stuffy. The people looked as wilted as the grass. And all the grass seemed to be private. Every time Eliza spotted a bush or green patch and walked Panda toward it, there were iron fences with signs on them.

RESIDENTS ONLY. NO BALL PLAYING. NO DOGS.

The sidewalks were crowded and dirty. Eliza began to look at everything from a dog's-eye view—one foot from the ground. London wasn't very glamorous at that level. The car noises were too loud and the smells too strong. Eliza spent hours in Hyde Park with bottles of mineral water, which she shared into a plastic dish for Panda, and with a Harrods rawhide chewing bone, which she let Panda have all to herself.

"There we were in Harrods, the best department store in the world," said Mom, "buying A RAWHIDE CHEWING BONE."

"It's the best rawhide chewing bone in the world," said Eliza. "Panda loves it."

Besides chewing on her rawhide bone, Panda began to learn some commands: sit, stay, fetch, down, and heel. She also developed a keen interest in pigeons. Pigeons were hard to herd. Every time Panda tried to round up the strays, they flew away in a circle.

"Here we are, a stone's throw from the greatest museums in the world, watching Panda herd pigeons in Hyde Park," said Mom.

"Museums get boring, Mom."

"Actually, the park can get pretty boring too, Eliza."

Yap, yap, yap, said Eliza, but she said it to herself, without even moving her lips. Eliza was never bored in the park. People stopped and spoke to Panda in lots of different languages. Several people offered to buy her. Others offered tips on how to train her. All of them declared her to be super or charming or delightful or adorable or friendly or intelligent or first-class. Eliza began collecting adjectives to modify Panda. In Ireland, sheepdogs were common. In London, they were a special item.

"Put on your sunblock, Eliza; you're going to get burned to a crisp."

"Mom, we're in London!"

"Eliza, sun is sun, and your skin is your skin. So here, put it on."

"Mom, I HATE sunblock. I HATE my skin."

"You have your father's skin, Eliza; it's lovely. It just happens to burn easily. Now put on your sunblock. No more arguing."

Eliza took the grungy little plastic bottle of sunblock and dabbed some on her nose.

"More."

More chore bore. Never, never, never in her whole life had Eliza once, ONCE, seen Mom make wonderful Mary put on sunblock. Mary used lotion, not block. Mary got lovely tans at the beach, where Eliza had to wear hats and long-sleeved shirts and towels wrapped around her legs like a mummy.

Eliza rubbed the leftover sunblock on her legs to get rid of the slimy feeling on her hands. Panda bounced over to investigate. Eagerly she began to lick off the sunblock.

"Mmmm. Sunblock number one hundred. Your favorite, Panda. Go for it."

"Eliza, I don't know whether that's good for her."

"If it's good for me, it's good for Panda. Live it up, Panda; we're in London."

The most important thing about London, besides keeping Panda happy, turned out to be meeting Queen Elizabeth. Not Queen Elizabeth II, but Queen Elizabeth I. Queen Elizabeth II was still alive, and boring. Queen Elizabeth I was dead and much more interesting.

Eliza met Queen Elizabeth I at Madame Tussaud's Wax Museum, where Mom took her while Dad Panda-sat. Eliza got to know Queen Elizabeth better at the Tower of London, where Dad took her while Mom Panda-sat. Queen Elizabeth's mother's head was cut off in the Tower, and Elizabeth herself was imprisoned there for a while. In addition to collecting adjectives to modify Panda, Eliza began collecting facts about Queen Elizabeth, also called Queen Bess, but not related to the highwayman's bonny sweetheart Bess.

The first important fact was that Queen Bess and Eliza had the same name, Elizabeth. Nicknames didn't count. Second of all, they both had red hair and waxy-white skin. *Put on your number one hundred sunblock this minute, Queen Elizabeth!* Actually, Queen Elizabeth's statue was made of wax, so maybe skin color didn't count. But third of all and most important, Queen Elizabeth's half sister was named Bloody Mary, who sounded much more interesting than Eliza's own wonderful half sister, Mary. Queen Elizabeth's half brother was a weak little boy who sounded easy to push around. Eliza longed for a weak little brother who was easy to push around. Mary could wrestle her to the floor with a headlock in one minute flat, not to mention outpitch, outrun, and outwit her.

"Look, Eliza, look at that bird in the window," Mary would say.

"Where? I don't see it."

"Oh, it flew away."

And Eliza would look back down at the table to find her chocolate cake gone.

"I'm going to do a report on Queen Elizabeth I this year," said Eliza one morning in the hotel breakfast room. Mom was upstairs puppy-sitting until Dad finished eating and took his turn on dog duty.

"You'll have your hands full with Queen Elizabeth I," said Dad. "She was a real character."

Eliza had once overheard two teachers talking about her in the hallway. "Eliza's a real character," one had said to the other. Eliza was not sure whether they meant good or bad, but if it was good enough for Queen Elizabeth I, it was good enough for her.

She began looking forward to going home, even if it meant starting school. The hotel where they were staying was tall, narrow, and carpeted all over. Eliza spent a lot of time scooping Panda up and running down four flights of stairs as soon as the puppy started sniffing in the corner.

"Fortunately, she's very particular about which part of the rug she pees on," said Mom. Before Panda could decide, Eliza made their quick exit outside. Her backyard in Chicago would be a lot more convenient. The flight was tomorrow, and Eliza could hardly wait. She felt jubilant because Panda could still squeeze into her box, even without being slicked with soap. And Mom had been able to upgrade their tickets because of all the traveling she did as a coach. If you traveled often enough and far enough with the same airline, the airline company gave you a bonus of free tickets or upgraded coach tickets to first class.

"Just think, folks, we'll be going first class!" said Mom. "I'll be glad for the extra room to stretch out these long legs."

Eliza was glad for the extra room for Panda's box. "No more growing tonight, Panda. We're on our way!"

"If we had stayed one more week," said Dad, "she would have been herding sheep in Ireland for the rest of her life."

"Lucky dog!" said Mom. "Herding sheep in Ireland beats not herding sheep in Chicago."

"Mom, we're trying to get her home!"

"How could I forget?"

Not only did Panda just manage to fit into the box, she also managed not to throw up in the taxi on the way to the airport, and she waited quietly in the long line for the security check. This time, Dad seemed to have the right information.

"I'll have to take her onto the plane for you," said the guard, "but she'll be waiting at your seat when you board. Just leave it to me." The guard's name tag said R. Sutton.

"Remember his name, Dad," Eliza whispered as the guard disappeared with the box.

"He seemed to know what he was doing," said Dad.

"I wish we were home already," said Eliza.

"Me too." Mom sighed. "I was looking forward to a first-class flight, but somehow I can't imagine it will be as restful with a puppy along."

The first thing that happened was that the flight attendant had to change their seats from the front row to one farther back so that Panda's box could be stowed safely under a seat ahead of them. This did not make the passengers who had just claimed those seats very happy, but they swapped anyway. It made Eliza extremely happy because now she could see the movie without getting a crick in her neck.

"Thanks, Panda," she whispered.

The displaced couple grumbled, Mom looked embarrassed, and Dad looked out the window. Soon the couple stopped glaring, however, because the flight attendant brought them some wine. By the time the engines started, she had brought them three glasses of wine each, and they were laughing out loud. Some of the other passengers frowned at Panda's box, but when she didn't move or make a sound, they forgot about her. Eliza did not.

"Mom, do you think she's still alive?" Eliza asked, peering into the box.

"She's sleeping, Eliza. Leave her alone. Hearing your voice may wake her up and get her excited."

The flight attendant brought a plateful of snacks for Eliza to choose from. They looked delicious until the attendant told her what they were. All of them sounded fishy and disgusting. Eliza took some melon balls. What a relief—the melon balls tasted sweet, Panda was peaceful, and the movie would start soon. In only eight hours, they would be home. Home sweet Chicago.

Eliza thought about her friends on the block and about Susie in her high-rise apartment. Panda and Sweetpea would be best friends, just like Eliza and Susie were. They could all go to the park and maybe the beach. Panda could learn how to do tricks just like Sweetpea—beg and roll over and shake hands. She could learn to fetch and maybe swim. Sheepdogs didn't like water much, but Panda would be different. The dog with a difference! Sweetpea and Panda could take baths together. Sweetpea got a bath every week. Her skin always gleamed pink under her snow-white fur.

After dinner, Eliza had trouble concentrating on the movie. It was boring anyway, with two people talking and kissing and talking and kissing and talking and kissing and nothing happening. Eliza felt restless. Her feet wiggled all by themselves and sometimes, by accident, poked the seat ahead of her. A tall man turned around and glared.

"Sit still, Eliza," Mom hissed.

The only place to go was the bathroom. It was not a thrilling bathroom, but Eliza went several times. Panda, on the other hand, had nowhere to go to the bathroom, which worried Eliza more and more as the plane droned on. What if Panda had an accident on the plane—peeyew. Better to think about Susie and Sweetpea and Panda and herself playing at the park. Better to drift off to sleep.

Suddenly the plane lurched. The seat-belt sign flashed on, and a deep voice came over the loudspeaker. "Folks, this is your captain speaking."

Dad gave Mom the "Oh, no" look.

"We're encountering some turbulence here, and we're going to have to ask you to sit down and buckle up. Nothing serious, but we're pushing against some heavy winds from Hurricane Deborah on the east coast of the U.S."

The plane continued to buck, while the attendant tried to keep from slopping coffee into people's laps. The captain's voice was drowned out by static on the intercom.

"Oh, great," muttered Eliza. "Now that I finally get a dog, we fall into the Atlantic Ocean."

"Be quiet, Eliza; I want to hear what he's saying," said Mom.

"There's really no safety problem here," continued the captain, "but we're using more fuel than we planned on our way to Chicago. We'll be landing in Bangor, Maine, for a refill, and those of you with connecting flights will have to add two hours to our flight time. We apologize for the delay but . . . better safe than sorry."

The plane heaved. Eliza thought she heard a whimper over the noise of the engines. She definitely heard the man in the seat ahead of her groan. Ha! Maybe he'd get sick. Mr. Grouch. The couple in the front row asked for two more glasses of wine. Eliza fingered her wart. Mom reached into her purse for Panda's pills.

"Wait," said Dad, putting his square hand over her

long fingers. "Let's wait and see if she really needs it."

"It's been a lot longer than three hours," said Mom anxiously. "I don't want her to start yelping."

"She's not bothering anybody, Mom," said Eliza. "Besides, too much medicine might make her sick."

Mom quickly took her hand out of her purse. The minutes dragged into hours. *Eliza and Panda struggled together in the cold Atlantic Ocean until they reached a life raft from their crashed plane. The hurricane winds swept them toward a deserted island and flung them up on the sand. For hours, Panda stood guard until Eliza regained consciousness. They managed to build a small shelter from the sticks that Panda retrieved along the shore, and they ate what they could forage. Panda hunted; Eliza did the fishing. Unlike the disgusting bits of fish on airplane trays, the fish Eliza caught tasted like spaghetti, a fish-wish dish.*

By the time the plane landed in Bangor, Maine, Panda was wide awake, but she still lay quiet except for a few cries when the pressure changed.

"Hurts her ears," said Dad.

"Mine too." Eliza winced.

Taking off again was not so bad, and the attendant produced more trays of food. Eliza remembered being younger and thinking that a breakfast flight meant you had to eat breakfast all the way—exactly what this flight felt like. Eliza was getting tired of eating and Panda was getting tired of not eating. The smell of food met with a polite whine in the area of Eliza's feet.

"Ten hours in a box, Panda. You're a hero," said Eliza as the plane finally jolted down on a runway at O'Hare Airport.

"She's a sheepdog," said Dad. "I told you she'd be calm."

Actually, thought Eliza, *I told you she'd be calm.* But she didn't say it out loud. While it was only 6:30 P.M. in Chicago, it was after midnight Irish time, and both her parents looked tired. Eliza, like Panda, was just getting waked up.

"Chicago, here we come," shouted Eliza as she carried Panda's box toward the terminal bus.

"Not so loud, Eliza," Mom grumped.

Eliza smiled to herself. Seven thousand miles, and she had a dog. First class.

6. Half Hound

Eliza, we have to get you new shoes before school starts."

Eliza was busy watching a show that their house sitter had taped while they were in Ireland. It was terrific to watch a late-afternoon show early in the morning. During the commercials, Eliza threw a ball for Panda. Panda caught the ball like a spider catches flies. She concentrated on Eliza's pitching hand and pounced on the ball as it flew through the air into her web of white teeth. *Snap trap.*

"Mom, it's too hot to go shopping."

"Look, Panda's chewed a hole in your sneakers."

"They look cool that way. I'll draw circles around the hole and it'll look like a whirlpool."

"Eliza, let's go."

"What about Susie?"

"What about Susie?"

"She was supposed to come over and play today."

"Eliza, we just got home from Ireland. I'm still jet-lagged, I have to start coaching tomorrow, and we have all your school stuff to get ready."

"What school stuff?"

"We have to fill out all those forms for after-school sports and get your allergy shots and everything."

"Yuck, after-school sports. Mom, do you realize that if you take the first letter of each word in after-school sports, it spells A-S-S, ass? I figured that out when we studied acronyms last year. Now everybody calls after-school sports ASS."

"Eliza, don't be crude."

"I'm not being crude. 'Ass' just means donkey. There are asses all over Ireland. There are even asses in the Bible. Anyway, Mom, I don't want to do after-school sports this year."

"What?"

"I DON'T WANT TO DO AFTER-SCHOOL SPORTS THIS YEAR."

"Don't shout, Eliza. Why not?"

"I just want to hang out with Panda and Susie and Sweetpea and the kids on the block after school. Between ASS and homework, I never have any time to play."

"You'll be bored in a week."

"I don't think so."

"You'll play Siamese twins with the TV."

"What does that mean?"

"Permanently attached."

"Mom, that's not funny."

"Probably not, but I'm not feeling funny. Anyway, you'll watch more TV than you do now, and you already watch too much TV."

"I don't, Mom."

"It cripples the imagination."

"It doesn't, Mom. My imagination is very healthy. My imagination loves television."

"That's what I'm afraid of. You won't be able to tell the difference between real and unreal."

"Mom."

Eliza watched her mother's mouth open and close like Panda panting in the heat—except that Mom kept barking about after-school dangers. *The masked man tied Eliza up, grabbed the TV set, and ran out the back door. Panda nosed the telephone closer to Eliza and began to gnaw on the ropes that bound her hands behind her back.*

"Who's going to take care of you after school?"

"Mom, I'll be ten years old next month. I can take care of myself. Besides, I have Panda now."

"Panda won't know what to do in an emergency."

"Dad will. I can call Dad in an emergency. He could get home in five minutes."

"We'll have to talk that over with him. Besides, Eliza, you're really getting to be a good basketball player. You need the practice, and you need the exercise, too. You've got so much energy I have to tackle you into bed every night. Plus, it's good discipline. Tell me the truth: Didn't you learn a lot from after-school sports last year?"

"Like what?"

"You tell me. What were the most important things you learned?"

"Oh, I learned to do pretty good jump shots in basketball, and I kick better in soccer now."

"What else?"

Eliza was quiet for a minute. "Well, I learned to love God."

"God? Really? How come?"

"That basketball player came and told us how he took drugs and drank and everything and it ruined his life and he could hardly play ball anymore and then he found God and he teaches sports camp now and he's really happy."

"Well, okay, that's one more thing."

"And I learned to love mud."

"Mud."

"Yeah, when it rained we went outside and ran around in the mud and it got real soft and slushy and felt like silk. Then we rubbed it on each other and drew pictures on the board fence around the playing field. It was better than anything else we did in ASS all year."

"Eliza, I don't know about this. Mary stayed in after-school sports till she was twelve years old. I worry about your being at loose ends all afternoon."

"Mom, I won't be at loose ends. I'll be PLAYING. I hate having to do the same thing at the same time every single day. Mary loves doing the same thing at the same time every single day. Besides, if I go to ASS, I won't have time to take care of Panda. You said she was all my responsibility."

"That's true, Eliza; I did."

"See? I have to come home and feed her and walk her and take her to the park."

"And clean up after her."

"Sure, and clean up after her."

"And do your homework."

"And do my homework. I'll have a lot more time for homework."

"All right, Eliza, we'll try it. But if it doesn't work out, you have to be willing to admit it and go back to after-school sports."

"Sure, Mom."

"Okay, now. Shoes."

Eliza decided not to resist shopping. She had won a major argument. Shoes were minor league. Anyway, it was hot. The dog days, Dad called them. It was not a good name for them. Panda hated heat. Eliza yearned for the cool rains of Ireland. She yearned for air-conditioning. Susie's new high-rise apartment was air-conditioned. Eliza's old wooden house was not. Panda lay on her side with her tongue hanging out, panting hard already even though it was early in the morning.

"You must be roasting in all that fur, Panda," said Eliza as she led the puppy down to the basement. Panda looked up at Eliza with sad eyes. The basement meant being locked up with a dish of water, a rawhide bone, and a wooden box with a pillow in it. Panda tried to dodge back up the stairs between Eliza's legs.

"No, you don't, Panda. Get down here. I'll be back as soon as I can. Stay! Good dog." Eliza could hear yips after she closed the door behind her.

"Mom, can't we bring her?"

"To the shoe store?"

"Sure; she'll be good."

"Ha! Ten pairs of shoes chewed through in ten minutes. An all-time record."

"Mom, you read too much sports news."

"No, Eliza. The answer is no."

"Okay, Mom, okay."

By the time they found a pair of shoes sensible enough to suit Mom and chic enough for Eliza, and then got the allergy shoes—which of course Mary never had to get because wonderful Mary wasn't allergic to anything—it was too late to ask Susie over because no one could drive her back and forth. Eliza rang several doorbells up and down the block, with no luck. Christine had to clean up her room. After that, Christine had to help her mother make cheerleaders' pom-poms. *Pom-poms? Pom-poms.* Christine's brother Christian was grounded. Matthew and Lauren were still at camp. Adam and Jacob were watching a movie and thought it was too hot to play outside. All the kids on the block came in pairs except Eliza. If only Mary hadn't stayed at college for a summer job, she'd be here to fight with. If only Mary were younger—and not so wonderful—Eliza would have a built-in companion. It wasn't fair. Everybody else was busy with something or somebody else. They acted like she hadn't been gone all summer. A couple of them acted like she didn't even exist. *Pom-poms!*

"Pom-poms," Eliza muttered on her way back home. With nobody around to see her, she played a quick game of hopscotch on her favorite patch of sidewalk. If they saw her, Christine and Christian and Matthew and Lauren and Adam and Jacob would tease her for playing hopscotch in public at the age of almost-ten, but personally, Eliza missed playing hopscotch in public.

"Nuts to everybody! I'll just take Panda to the park by myself." She and Mom and Dad had agreed that IF she crossed at the light and IF she stayed on the hill with the other dog walkers and IF she didn't talk to strangers and IF she went before dark, it was safe for her to take Panda to the park by herself. It seemed like a lot of ifs. Four. Four ifs. There were no such ifs in Ireland. You just went out with your dog.

Eliza brought the rope to play tug-of-war in the park, but Panda was too distracted by all the sights and sounds to pay much attention. Most of the other dog walkers weren't home from work yet, and the dogs that were there looked rough—a German shepherd and a Doberman were both straining at their leashes.

Eliza was about to turn toward home when suddenly Panda lunged forward, jerking her leash out of Eliza's hand and streaking toward a little boy whose father had just thrown him a ball. A look of terror spread across the child's face as he started running toward his father.

"Panda!" screamed Eliza.

Joyfully, Panda hurtled herself after the ball and the little boy, who tripped and fell and tried to scramble up again. Distracted from the ball, Panda threw herself on him and licked his muddy legs, but he cried and squirmed away. Eliza and his father reached him at the same time. Eliza grabbed Panda's collar as the man snatched up his son, cradling him high out of Panda's reach.

"Bad dog!" Eliza yelled at Panda. "BAD DOG!"

The little boy cried into his father's shoulder. "The mean dog hurted me . . . the mean dog hurted me," he sniffled over and over.

Eliza felt close to tears herself as the man turned his back and stalked away, comforting his son.

"I'm sorry," she called after them. "I'm really sorry. She wouldn't have hurt you. She's just a puppy." The man did not even look back at her. There was no one to comfort Eliza—except Panda. She wagged her tail at Eliza and pulled her along, ready for another game. Eliza walked slowly, replaying the boy's tears and cries over and over. The sidewalk felt like a hot stove. When they got to Eliza's gate, Panda was eager to go in, but Eliza tugged her on.

"No, Panda, you haven't pooped yet. Come on; we're going to walk to the end of the block."

Panda walked a few slow steps, pulled back on her leash, and flopped down on her stomach. Her back legs stretched flat, and she dropped her nose on her front paws. Her eyes rolled up to Eliza as if to say, "No more." Just like Mom's. Eliza picked up the puppy and carried her farther down the block.

"There now, Panda. You are going to do what you are supposed to do. You may not know what that is yet, but you better learn." Panda did what she was supposed to do. So did Eliza. She whipped out her plastic Baggie. *Ladies and gentlemen, you see before you the perfect puppy pooper picker upper!* Eliza tried to say "perfect puppy pooper picker upper" out loud ten times in a row as fast as she could. It was better than "pick a peck of pickled peppers."

They walked into the garden just as Dad approached the gate.

"Hi, Dad." Eliza ran back and gave him a hug. He turned to watch Panda snuffle up and down the garden path as if her nose were attached to the flat stones.

"She's half hound," laughed Dad. "Looks like she's sniffing rabbit tracks."

Panda stuck her nose into a wild strawberry plant and ate the red berries that had ripened late under the leaves.

"Can you believe that? I wondered where all the strawberries were going," said Dad. "I thought you had picked them when we got home."

"No, I didn't even get one. I thought they had dried up and fallen off. Panda, you're a pig."

"She's a rascal. We should have named her Pan, for the god of mischief."

"Panda would have to be a goddess, Dad."

"Well, maybe Pandora then. She let all kinds of mischief loose in the world. Where's your mother?" Dad unlocked the door and led Eliza toward the kitchen. Panda followed with a strawberry leaf hanging from one side of her mouth.

"Mom's running. She said she had to get back in shape again to set a good example for the team."

"She's brave to run in this heat."

"Mom Pom-pom the Perfect," muttered Eliza, rubbing her wart. Would this wart ever give up?

"What did you say, Eliza?"

"Nothing, Dad."

"Did you say Mom was perfect?"

"No, Dad, just kidding."

"That's bordering on insolence, Eliza Daly."

"I'm sorry, Dad."

"Mom does try too hard sometimes, Eliza. It's hard to be a woman in athletics. You know that. And it was a lot harder when she was a girl. She got where she is by doing her best all the time. You have to understand that."

"I do, Dad. It's just that she wants me to be that way too."

"She pushes herself harder than she pushes you, believe me, Eliza. And you're a lot more like her than you know. You and Mary both take after your mother. And you're both wonderful girls. Now bring me a can of tomatoes for the spaghetti sauce."

Eliza retrieved the can of tomatoes in stunned silence. No one had ever called her wonderful before. Mary was wonderful, but she could never keep up with Mary. Of course, Mary was twenty years old. No wonder Eliza couldn't keep up with Mary. *This is my wonderful daughter Mary, and this is my wonderful daughter Eliza,* said Mom to her *star basketball players. "They are ten years apart but equally wonderful."* Wow, wonderful Eliza!

She did a wonderful-Eliza dance all around the kitchen.

"Watch out, Eliza; you're going to trip over something and fall down."

Suddenly, like a small ghost of memory from the park, the little boy fell down again. *The mean dog hurted me . . . the mean dog hurted me.* Eliza no longer felt wonderful. *I told you this dog was too much, Eliza. You can't handle everything by yourself. Go back to after-school sports.*

While Dad dumped the can of tomatoes into a pan and started adding herbs, Eliza told him about what had happened in the park. Panda played with an ice cube from

Eliza's water glass, batting it across the floor, tossing it into the air, and cracking it in her teeth.

"You've got a big job ahead of you, Eliza, with Panda to train and school starting tomorrow."

"I can do it, Dad; you'll see. I can hardly wait. The first thing I'm going to do is write a report about Panda."

"I thought you were going to write a report on Queen Elizabeth I."

"Well, one or the other."

"There's quite a difference . . . although, come to think of it, they both got into trouble as youngsters."

"Half of it was my fault, Dad. I should have held her leash tighter."

"Queen Elizabeth's?"

"Dad."

Eliza's father leaned over to ruffle Panda's ears. "Pandemonium—half demon, half hound."

"But mine, Dad, all mine."

7. Capital Canine

Getting up for school, after a long summer off, was hard work. Dad came in three times to wake her. Every time, Eliza felt sleep pull her back into deep, downy darkness. Then she heard a roar from the stairs.

"Eliza, get up this minute! I better not have to come in there again." Dad didn't shout very often, but he had been in the marines and had strong ideas about getting up early. Mom had not been in the marines but had so much energy that she got up early anyway. Eliza had not been in the marines and she spent all of her energy putting off bedtime, so she was always tired early in the morning.

The first day of school was exciting enough to get up for.

The second day was okay.

The second week started dragging. There were so many sheets of information to bring home for her parents that Eliza felt like a walking newspaper. Most of the information was boring: where to pick up your child for car pools, how much money to send for milk, who to call in case your child got sick. Eliza's least favorite was the louse note: "We have had reports of head lice in Mrs. Dow's fifth grade. Tonight carefully inspect your child's hair, especially around the ears and the nape of the neck, in good light."

Mom took apart Eliza's head, hair by hair. Fortunately, she found nothing. If she had, the note suggested placing toys in plastic bags and sealing them tightly for at least ten days. What about Panda? *Seal your dog tightly for ten days. Should your dog need to breathe, eat, or go to the bathroom, disregard any signs of distress. Remember, after ten days, your dog will be lice-free.* Eliza vowed never to share her comb with anyone.

After the louse note, the teachers settled down to business. Mrs. Dow cornered Eliza right after sustained Silent Reading for a student-teacher conference. Student-teacher conferences often meant that parent-teacher conferences might come next, so Eliza listened carefully.

"What have you been reading lately, Eliza?" she asked.

"*Asterix.*"

"No, I mean in Sustained Silent Reading."

"I've been reading *Asterix* in Sustained Silent Reading."

"Don't you think you're ready for something more challenging than comic books?"

"I could bring in my *Tin Tins*. They're a lot harder to read."

"Actually, Eliza, I was thinking you might want to start reading for your report. Some of the other students have already begun. Have you chosen a topic?"

"Either Border collies or Queen Elizabeth I."

"Now Eliza, I understand from your other teachers that you've reported on dogs every year."

"This would be different. This would be on a particular kind of dog."

"Why don't you try something completely different, Eliza. Try Queen Elizabeth I."

"I wonder if she had a dog?"

"That would certainly be worth checking into, but it might not be the most important aspect of her reign. What interests you about Queen Elizabeth?"

"Well, we have the same name, for one thing. For another thing, she was a real character. I think Queen Elizabeth was . . ." Eliza hesitated.

"Yes?"

"Queen Elizabeth was like me, in some ways."

"I'll be curious to find out how, Eliza. It would be a good idea for you to start with the encyclopedia for some general facts and then go to the library. I'm sure you can find a biography of Queen Elizabeth. And Eliza, don't forget we have a test on the state capitals next week."

Eliza stared at the picture of the polar bears on the wall. Next to dogs, she loved bears best. Maybe that's why Panda had seemed so special right from the first—dog and panda bear combined. Eliza had never seen a panda bear, but the Lincoln Park Zoo had polar bears. She and Mary had watched them rolling around in the snow. "Aren't they freezing to death?" Eliza had asked.

"We're talking blubber, Eliza," Mary had answered. "Heavy blubber."

Sometimes Eliza missed Mary. Eliza missed Panda every minute at school.

"Eliza?"

Eliza turned to see Mrs. Dow staring at her.

"The test on state capitals next week?"

"Right, Mrs. Dow; I remember."

"And the library, Eliza. Right now would be a good time to go down to the library for some information on Queen Elizabeth."

"Right, Mrs. Dow." *Pow. Dow cow plow.* Mrs. Dow

reminded Eliza of Mom, plowing ahead, always sure she was right.

But Mom had been wrong about after-school sports. Eliza loved after-school without sports. It was true that most of the neighborhood kids were too busy with music lessons or day-care arrangements or homework to play much, and Susie lived too far away to get together, but Panda was always waiting for her.

When Eliza came home from school that day and opened the basement door, Panda danced circles around her, jumped up and down, rolled over, dashed out the back door as soon as Eliza opened it, peed, raced back inside, and wagged her tail wildly.

"Panda, you're going to sprain your tail," said Eliza. Panda's tongue lolled out in a doggy grin. Two of her puppy teeth had fallen out, and she looked gummy. Eliza tossed her a dog biscuit, made herself a mug of chocolate milk, and peeled a banana. Panda chomped down the dog biscuit, pulled her leash off the hook, dragged it over to Eliza's feet, and dropped it on the floor.

"All right, all right, we'll go to the park. Just wait till I finish my snack."

Panda bounced over to the couch and trotted back with a tennis ball.

"Panda, we're going, okay? Just relax."

As soon as they started off to the park, Panda took charge, straining at the leash like a husky pulling a sled. Eliza was developing a lot of sympathy for sleds. She knew how they felt. At the edge of the park, Eliza let Panda go. Panda no longer chased children or hid between Eliza's legs when other dogs came near. Panda had a little more control of herself, and she had made some friends. She pranced up to them like a queen to swap sniffs. On good days, the hill in the park was a dog circus. Eliza arranged the performers in alphabetical order. Alice the basset hound, Bailey the weimaraner, Buck the white Labrador, Cleopatra the malamute, Elliott the beagle, Humphrey the Old English sheepdog, Jake the black Labrador, Petey the West Highland terrier, Reebock the golden retriever, and Sheba the Jack Russell terrier. They romped and tussled and slobbered and chewed each others' ears.

Watching the dogs run around was different from watching the classroom hamsters run around. The hamsters ran endlessly on a wheel, like after-school sports—like Eliza trying to keep up with Mary. Or sometimes the hamsters tried to dig out of the bottom of their exercise box and escape, while Eliza made sure they didn't succeed. Hamster watching was a lonely business compared to dog walking. Thanks to Panda, Eliza had a lot of new friends. The dog people liked Panda. They said she was quick and intelligent. In the darkening fall afternoons, they said her white legs looked like flashlights. They said she was the best ball chaser in the park.

"My mom thinks she's a little hyperactive," said Eliza.

"She'll settle down," said Humphrey's owner. "Humphrey was a different dog after he turned seven months old."

Humphrey was gnawing on Panda's head.

"Why don't you take her to the Tail Waggers Club dog-obedience classes? They were a big help to Humphrey and me. Come on, Humphrey; it's time to go home."

Humphrey lumbered after Panda, who had just escaped his jaws and was running circles around him, inviting another attack.

"Humphrey, COME!"

Humphrey pounced on Panda.

"Humphrey, come NOW!" Humphrey's owner pulled a dog biscuit out of her pocket. Humphrey appeared instantly at her side.

"Good dog. See how obedient he is? Those Tail Waggers Club dog-obedience classes are wonderful." Humphrey's owner clicked the leash onto Humphrey's collar. Humphrey balked. The dog biscuit was gone, and

Panda was still there. Humphrey's owner pulled one way and Humphrey pulled another. It was a fairly even match. Humphrey was a very large dog, and Humphrey's owner was a very small woman. Slowly, she wrestled him down the hill. Eliza was lucky to have a medium-small dog. *"More medium than small, if you ask me," said Mom.*

One by one, the other dog owners left until Eliza was alone with her medium-small dog. She threw the ball for a while and Panda herded it back. On the other side of the hill, where everybody sledded in winter, two boys raced their bikes. Halfway down, they jumped the wheels like skiers flying through the air. Then they landed and pushed the bikes back up and roared down again. Eliza could picture herself doing exactly the same thing. *All of the dog people in Oz Park gathered to watch Panda's owner speed-thrill down the hill. They held their breaths as she poised her bike at the top of the steep slope for a trial run. Five times she took the hill, flying downward with the grace of a champion skier, her black-and-white Border collie streaking by her side.*

The faster Eliza imagined peddling her bike, the faster she threw the ball. Panda was panting hard when they headed back to the house.

During homework breaks, Eliza lay down on the floor, put the ball on her stomach, and, with the help of seventeen dog biscuits, taught Panda how to jump over the ball and her body. Step two was getting Panda to jump over a stick, which Eliza planned to raise higher and higher until Panda became a champion jumper.

Eliza no longer envied Susie for having a bichon frise. Susie had brought Sweetpea over to the house once. The two dogs did not play. Sweetpea seemed nervous compared to Panda. Sweetpea's toenails kept going click-click-click across the floor. Sweetpea also, Eliza had to admit, yapped. While Panda romped and tussled with the rope or dropped off to sleep with all four paws up in the air above her spotted stomach or flopped under a chair with a WHUFF, Sweetpea's toenails still clicked. Click-click-click, click-click-click, click-click-click. Eliza had never known how extremely annoying nonstop toenail clicks could be. So Mom could be right sometimes. But not as often as she thought.

"Right, Mom," said Eliza that night at the dinner table. Dad had fixed "meatbulbs," the family code for meatballs, which Eliza had not been able to pronounce clearly at an earlier stage of her life. Like about two years old. She wished Mom and Dad would switch from "meatbulbs" back to "meatballs" now. Maybe they had forgotten the real word.

"Right, Mom, we do have some homework. I have to

learn the state capitals."

"All of them?"

"All of them."

"By when?"

"Next week."

"That doesn't give you much time, Eliza."

"I know the capital of Illinois already."

"You have a long way to go. Fifty states in five days. That's ten capitals a night."

"Minus one."

"Well, you'd better get busy. What else?"

"I have to work on my report about Queen Elizabeth."

"What have you found out so far?" asked Dad.

"King Henry VIII had Elizabeth's mother beheaded after their marriage was declared dull and void."

"Null and void, Eliza, not dull and void. It might have been dull, too, but 'null' means 'nothing.' Their marriage was canceled."

"How can you cancel a marriage?"

"That's what King Henry VIII spent six wives trying to figure out. He finally worked out a system for divorce, but some of his wives lost their heads in the process."

Both of Eliza's parents had been divorced before they married each other. She did not want to think about it. Quickly, she switched thoughts before her parents' ex-wife's and ex-husband's heads could roll across the floor. She reached down to pat Panda under the table. Panda was hoping for another meatbulb. Eliza had dropped a piece, entirely by accident. After that, Panda watched Eliza with devoted attention.

"Could we rent a movie tonight?"

"Certainly not, Eliza. It's a school night," said Mom. "You're going to bed early so you won't be tired in the morning."

"Mom, if I go to bed early, I just lie there and can't sleep and I'm still tired in the morning but I haven't had any fun."

"You can read a book."

"Can I be excused now?"

"No, stay and talk with us for a while," said Dad.

Eliza wished Mary were home. Then she could slip away unnoticed and watch her favorite show, which was just about to come on any minute, and wonderful Mary would do all the talking. Mary really was wonderful at some things, and keeping her parents occupied was one of them. When Eliza wanted attention, it wasn't so wonderful to have Mary getting it, but when Eliza didn't want attention, Mary was very handy. Dinner should be for eating, mostly dessert, not yap-yap-yapping.

"Did you have any fights today, Eliza?" asked Mom.

"Mom, I don't fight at school anymore. I just had a little argument with Joshua, and a little tiny one with Laura."

"How come?"

"Laura left her pencil on my desk and wouldn't pick it up at clean-up time."

"How did you know it was hers?"

"I could tell it was Laura's pencil because of the bite marks."

"You keep dental records on your friends?" asked Dad.

"No, but Laura bites on everything. She used to bite me in preschool."

"What was the other fight?" asked Mom suspiciously.

"It wasn't a fight, Mom. Joshua just kept annoying me."

"How come?"

"First he slapped me. Then he said how much he liked me. Then he slapped me again. Then I kicked him in the shins. Then he stopped."

"Which Joshua is this?"

"Joshua Houple. I like the other Joshua. He's careful about how I feel and he never burps."

"The other Joshua sounds like a real gentleman. How do you like Mrs. Dow?"

"She's fine. She smells like strawberries."

"Eliza, you're half hound too," said Dad. Then he had

to tell Mom about Panda eating the strawberries, which Eliza already knew. Dad liked to tell the same story over and over and over.

"So you're not getting bored alone after school?" Mom asked.

"I'm not alone, Mom. Panda's with me, and there's lots to do. We're going to bike to the park tomorrow," said Eliza.

"Well, be careful," said Mom.

"We're just going to bike down the hill."

"I don't think that's such a good idea."

"All the kids do it, Mom."

"It sounds risky to me. You're so headlong, Eliza."

"My head is not long!"

"'Headlong' means 'impetuous, impulsive.' You throw yourself into things without thinking. I'm afraid you'll have an accident."

"Mom, I sled down that hill every year."

"That's different. Snow is soft when you fall, and you're close to the ground. Falling off a bike could be really dangerous."

"I have a helmet, Mom. Now can I be excused?" asked Eliza.

"All right, but only if you work on those capitals," said Mom. "I'm going to check you on ten every night this week."

"Every night?"

"Every night."

"Weekends?"

"Eliza, get on with it," said Mom. "And take Panda out in the backyard. She just farted."

"MOM."

"Well, that's what she did. Now scoot."

Eliza practiced ten capitals out loud to Panda. "Springfield, Illinois; Montgomery, Alabama; Juneau, Alaska; Phoenix, Arizona; Little Rock, Arkansas; Sacramento, California; Denver, Colorado; Hartford, Connecticut; Dover, Delaware; Tallahassee, Florida." Tallahassee was her favorite so far. It rhymed with Lassie.

That night Eliza could not sleep. After Panda was shut into the basement and Eliza was shut into bed, she kept saying the ten capitals in her head. Finally Mom came into her room to check on her before settling into bed herself. Dad was already snoring.

"Eliza, this room is a mess. There's stuff all over the floor."

"I like it that way, Mom. It keeps me in shape for hopscotch. Every day, I play secret hopscotch over the stuff on my floor. And don't ever ever ever tell Susie, or she'll tell everybody else I act like a baby and I'll die."

"Well, someday you're going to land on your head

instead of your feet if you're not careful. Tomorrow I want you to clean up this room. Right now it's time for you to go to sleep."

"I can't sleep," complained Eliza.

"How come?"

"My leg won't hold still."

"Eliza, I've heard some good ones, and you yourself have done better."

"No, really, Mom, my leg wiggles all by itself. It's restless. Could you say 'The Highwayman' for me?"

"I don't know 'The Highwayman,' Eliza; that's your father's trick. Say the capitals in your head."

"I tried that."

"Try it again. Catch a kiss, now, Sweetpea, and get to sleep."

"Mom, Sweetpea is a dog."

"I was calling you Sweetpea long before I met that bichon frise, Eliza."

"Mom, do you think dogs get warts?"

"I don't know, Eliza."

"Do you think Queen Elizabeth had any warts?"

"Good night, Eliza."

"Good night, Mom. Don't turn out your light till I fall asleep."

"Fall asleep, Eliza."

In the dim night light, Eliza stared at the Styrofoam porcupine she had made in preschool. With only two toothpicks left and a squiggly face drawn with Magic Marker, it looked like something from the evolution play her class had done last year; Joshua had played a sponge, and Laura had played a volcano. Dressed in a kangaroo costume, Eliza had shown the progress of mammals along an imaginary time line. All baby stuff—like "meatbulbs" for "meatballs," or "dull and void" for "null and void." Well, nobody's perfect. A million years ago, Eliza used to confuse "masculine" with "muscular." Dad corrected her about the words and Mom about the concept. "You know females can be muscular, Eliza." Yes, she knew that. Her mother was muscular. Her mother worked out in the gym with a friend who was a stockbroker, and Eliza had once called him a "stockbreaker," which everyone thought was very funny. It was not very funny. It was very logical. If he had finished breaking stocks, then he would be a stockbroker. Even word makers were not perfect.

The night light wavered. "The wind was a torrent of darkness among the gusty trees." The highwayman galloped past as sleep pulled her into deep, downy darkness. *Good night, moon; room; Mom; Dad; Mrs. Dow; Mary; Queen Elizabeth; the highwayman; Panda; Sweetpea; Irish donkeys across the sea; Susie; Joshua; Laura; Springfield, Illinois;*

Montgomery, Alabama; Juneau, Alaska; Phoenix, Arizona; Little Rock, Arkansas; Sacramento, California; Denver, Colorado; Hartford, Connecticut; Dover, Delaware; Tallahassee Lassie, Florida; meatbulbs; muscular; stockbusters; everybody. Especially Panda, capital canine, most missed, deep down in the basement. Calling Panda, capital of the basement . . . this is Eliza, capital of the bed. I am lonely.

8. Demon Dog

Eliza to the rescue!" shouted Eliza. Every morning when she opened the basement door, Panda went bananas with happiness. Her whole body curled back and forth, from tongue to tail. She panted her doggy smile and curled in circles and chased Eliza's feet into the kitchen.

Mom was drinking coffee and reading the sports pages. Eliza sat down across from Mom and rubbed Panda's ears.

"Mom, you know how my birthday is coming up soon?"

"Yes, Eliza."

"You know what I really want?"

"I thought you wanted a dog."

"Yes, but what else I really want, now that I already have a dog and she's such a good dog?"

"What?"

"Really really really really really reallyreallyreallyreally reallyreallyreallyreally want?"

"Eliza, I have to go to work. I'm running late already."

"You know how Panda always has to sleep in the basement?"

"Yes, Eliza. Here, put a juice carton in your lunch. And turn off that television. It's driving me crazy."

"Dad's watching the morning news."

"Take him the newspaper. I have to have some quiet with my coffee."

"Well, for my birthday, I want Panda to be able to sleep in my room at night."

Panda perked up her ears at the sound of her name and pranced around the kitchen, looking for some cheese.

"She hasn't had one single accident in the basement," said Eliza.

"She's waiting to get up to your room," said Mom.

"Mom, Border collies are smarter than other dogs. They train quicker. Panda's not going to have any accidents anywhere."

"Eliza, this is not a good time for an argument."

"I'm not arguing, Mom."

"Okay, for a discussion of this nature."

"It's not exactly a discussion, Mom; it's a request. A birthday request. For my tenth birthday."

"We'll see."

Step number one. Mom did not say no.

In school, Eliza gazed at the blackboard. Black and white. *Panda curled up close beside her in bed. They made a nest of the covers, soft and warm. When the cold winds blew and the wolves howled, Panda lifted her head alertly but never left Eliza's side.*

"How are you coming on your capitals, Eliza?" asked Mrs. Dow.

"Capitals?"

"Are you practicing your capitals?"

"Every night." *Every night Panda kept her company in the long dark hours and listened to the capitals, ears cocked, punctuating each capital with soft little barks. Slowly Eliza began to realize how truly intelligent a Border collie could be. Her dog was learning the capitals. One bark for Springfield, Illinois. Two barks for Montgomery, Alabama. Three barks for Juneau, Alaska . . . Good dog, Panda!*

Mrs. Dow was staring at her again. "Eliza, we were discussing your assignments. Have you made some progress on your Queen Elizabeth report?"

"Queen Elizabeth?"

"Queen Elizabeth!"

"I read the encyclopedia."

"Well, you need to find some other sources too. The encyclopedia is oversimplified sometimes. It can make even the most complex subjects seem black and white."

"Black and white?"

"Eliza, you sound like an echo chamber today. Yes, black and white—you know what I mean: clearly one way or the other—when in fact Queen Elizabeth did a lot of compromising. She was too colorful a character to fit into neat little black-and-white patterns."

Black-and-white patterns. What was wrong with black-and-white patterns? Panda had neat little black-and-white patterns, and the amazing thing was that the patterns weren't just on her fur. They went all the way through to her skin. Through the thin fur on her pink stomach, you could see beautiful patches of actual black-and-white skin. She was a Designer Dog through and through, a true-blue Designer Dog, a true-blue black-and-white Designer Dog. Eliza was learning a lot more about dogs from Panda than she had from the dog encyclopedia, which never said anything about how black-and-white fur patterns were skin-deep. Maybe encyclopedias were oversimplified. In fact, Panda was a lot more interesting than the dog encyclopedia. She was even more interesting than the *Lassie* reruns. Eliza wondered if Panda would save her from a burning building.

Flames crackled all around. Smoke rose in clouds, filling Eliza's bedroom on the second floor. Panda barked and barked at the basement door. Finally, she stood on her hind feet with her front feet leaning against the door, chomped down on the doorknob with her teeth, and turned the knob. The door swung open. Heat engulfed her, but she raced toward the stairs that led to Eliza's room. Another closed door. Panda reared up and opened this one the same way. Eliza opened her eyes to stinging smoke, a wet tongue, and a snuffling nose. "Quick, Panda, wake up Mom and Dad." The fire roared.

"Eliza?"

"Yes, Mrs. Dow?"

"The bell has rung."

"Oh."

"Some time ago."

"Oh."

"School is out for the day."

"Oh."

"Hurry, or you'll miss your bus. And don't forget your homework."

"Yap, yap, yap," Eliza mumbled very softly. She hated getting left in the middle of a burning building.

When the bus dropped her off at home, Eliza was a little surprised to find the house looking peaceful. No smoke or flames poured from the windows. Panda did her dog dance and waited for Eliza to get the leash.

"We're going to bike in the park today, Panda. You'll get a good run, and I can speed-thrill down the hill." Mom didn't want Eliza to speed-thrill down the hill, but she hadn't absolutely said no. Step number one.

Eliza looked for her helmet but couldn't find it. Panda whined and danced. She needed to get out fast. *There's no way that dog can sleep all night in your room, Eliza, if she's still having accidents during the daytime!* With pooper bags, the bike, and the leash—which Panda pulled on hard toward the park—Eliza had her hands full, but she was careful to walk across the street guiding her bike with one hand and her dog with the other so that neither would get hurt in the traffic.

In the middle of the park, she unleashed Panda and pushed her bike slowly up the hill. When she got to the top, she turned around. It was a long way down. None of the dog people were around yet, so she had plenty of time to practice. "Ready, Panda?" she called. Then she pushed off as hard as she could with a running start and leaped onto the seat.

The bike sped down the hill. So did Panda. The bike

looked like a mechanical sheep, like a wild stray running away with Eliza down the hill. Panda ran faster to head off the danger. As she cut in front of the mechanical sheep, her tail tangled with the front wheel and she began to yelp. Eliza jammed on the handle brakes as hard as she could. With a sudden jerk, the bicycle stopped near the bottom of the hill. Eliza kept going. Her body sailed over the top of the handlebars, and her head hit the pavement with a crunch.

Eliza woke up on the sidewalk with Panda licking her face. Panda must be okay. But Eliza's head hurt so badly that she felt like throwing up. She definitely did not feel like moving. Tears began rolling down her face, all by themselves. Panda licked more frantically. Suddenly a woman's face appeared where Panda's had been, and another furry face appeared beside Panda's. Humphrey!

"Are you okay?" Humphrey's owner asked.

"I don't think so," Eliza said. Even her tongue hurt.

Humphrey began to lick Eliza's hand, which still tasted like after-school snack. Humphrey's tongue covered her whole hand with one lick. Eliza felt very tired. She felt like going to sleep right there on the sidewalk, with Panda licking her face and Humphrey licking her hand.

"Your name is Eliza, right? I saw you fall from across

the park. You landed on your head. Lie still, now; you've got a real bruise and bump there, and it's bleeding some. I'm going to help you get home. Can you tell me where you live?"

Eliza tried to remember where she lived. It was right across the street and around the corner. She pointed.

"Okay, my car's parked nearby. Just stay right here, and I'll be back."

Eliza could not imagine going anywhere. Her mind was stuck on replay. The green grass of the hill flew by her over and over, with Panda's tail tangled in her bike wheel in a blur of black-and-white yelps.

Somehow Humphrey's owner got Eliza into her tiny car, along with huge Humphrey and panting Panda, and Eliza found her keys in her pocket, and Humphrey's owner called her father from the emergency list by the telephone. Somehow, Eliza found herself in a white bed in a white room with her mother and father beside her, a needle in her arm, and a lot of machines thumping away.

She was sleepy, so sleepy, but her mother kept talking to her.

"Don't go to sleep, Eliza. You've had a concussion, and you need to stay awake."

"Yap, yap, yap," said Eliza.

"What?"

Her mother did not seem to understand anything Eliza said. Or was Eliza just thinking what she said and not really saying it out loud? Eliza looked out the window. Carefully she opened her mouth and said, very loud, "It's dark outside. You wanted me to go to bed early."

"Not tonight, Eliza. You get to stay up all night."

"Can I watch TV?" asked Eliza.

"Yes," said Mom and Dad at the same time. Eliza could hardly believe her ears. She tried to sit up. Dad put his hand against her shoulder.

"Stay put, honey; you're all hooked up. They hang the TVs near the ceiling so you don't have to sit up. You're going to be fine, but they're going to keep you in intensive care for the night just to make sure. This is a heart monitor. That's some kind of solution they're dripping into your bloodstream to keep you shipshape."

"I'm sorry for what happened," Eliza whispered.

"Oh, Eliza," said Mom. "We heard about it from the woman in the park. I don't understand how you could—"

"Let's talk about it later," said Dad, "when Eliza feels better."

For once, Eliza was glad to wait. She looked down at the tape over her arm and listened to the beeps around her. Then she looked up at the clock. It was time for her favorite rerun, *Mr. Ed.* They watched it together. Mom rolled her eyes a couple of times, but she didn't say it was dumb. Dad even laughed. Then they watched two of her other favorite reruns, *Get Smart* and *The Donna Reed Show.*

"These are pretty old shows," said Mom.

"You told me old things are valuable, Mom."

"Well, some old things are."

"These old black-and-white shows are the best," said Dad.

"Black and white," mumbled Eliza.

"What?"

"Nothing."

"Are you feeling okay?"

"Yeah, just a headache."

Then they watched reruns of *Different Strokes, The Cosby Show,* and a talk show—all in color. Except for the headache, Eliza felt like she was in heaven. Her eyes did feel heavy, though, and her head thundered as if the highwayman were pounding through it. A young doctor came by and checked her and said she could sleep if Dad or Mom woke her up every half hour. She heard Mom and Dad dividing up the night, Dad with the first shift and Mom with the next.

The night passed full of beeps and lights and buzzers and crying from a baby Eliza couldn't see and the face of her father who stroked her cheek every half hour till she opened her eyes for a few minutes. Then it was her mother's face. Her mother was reading a book.

"Mom, where's Panda?"

"She's at home in the basement, where she belongs."

"Mom, it wasn't her fault."

"Whose was it?"

"It was just an accident."

"Eliza, you could have been killed. I told you how dangerous it is to bike down that hill."

"I shouldn't have gone without my helmet, Mom. I'll never do it again."

Mom didn't say anything. Her mouth was closed tight. Her eyes had black circles under them. Finally she sighed. "It was a mistake to leave you on your own after school, Eliza."

"No, Mom, I've been doing fine. I've taken care of my dog and done my homework every day like I promised. I just made one mistake."

"One mistake is enough."

"Mom, you make everything so black and white."

"Some things are black and white, Eliza."

"But everybody makes mistakes, Mom. I still have to try things. I'll try harder if you let me try again. We have to compromise. It's like Queen Elizabeth. Mrs. Dow said even Queen Elizabeth had to compromise."

Mom sighed. "Eliza, I think you're feeling better."

"I am, Mom. I want to go home. I miss Panda."

"We can't go home yet. The doctor has to discharge you

first. And you're going to miss some school. The doctor said you'd have to stay quiet in bed for a while."

"Can Panda stay quiet with me? Even at night? My birthday's so close. It could be an early present."

"We'll see, Eliza. I'll talk it over with your father."

Step number two.

That night, Panda snuggled on top of the down comforter while Eliza scratched her ears. "Demon dog," she said softly, "you got me into a lot of trouble. But you didn't mean to. You're lucky you didn't get a tail concussion. I bet you'll never chase a bicycle again. I bet this wart will never go away. I bet you don't even care if it does or not."

Panda was shedding her soft puppy fur. Her long adult coat was a little stiffer. The creamy tan bits under her ears had darkened. "See, Panda, not everything is black and white," she whispered into Panda's ear. "Some things are brown."

Panda shook her head. She did not care for hot air in her ear. Then she folded her plumy tail over her sharp nose, sighed contentedly, and went to sleep on Eliza's bed.

It was better than the basement.

9. Royal Dog

For her birthday, Eliza got furry black-and-white slippers with toes shaped like dalmatians. ("They didn't have any Border collies," said Mom.) She also got an after-concussion headache, but that didn't count. She got a rubber-stamp-and-ink kit that made paw marks on paper, a gift certificate for the Tail Waggers Club dog-obedience classes, a copy of Elvis Presley's hit single "You Ain't Nothin' but a Hound Dog," and a big, framed photograph of Panda, the first one they had taken in Ireland. Looking at the picture made Eliza realize how much her puppy had grown.

"Leggy," said the vet, when he examined her for the last round of booster shots. Any dog participating in the Tail Waggers Club obedience classes had to have shots and worm pills. The Tail Waggers Club was the best present because Dad was going to drive both Eliza and Susie to the weekly classes. Panda and Sweetpea would learn how to behave together.

"Panda already knows how to sit," said Eliza.

"Basically, she knows dog biscuits," said Dad. He was peeling potatoes for dinner. "She's got to obey whether or not you're carrying Chunky Chews in your pocket."

"She does, Dad."

"Sometimes."

"Nobody's perfect."

"We're looking for a Hank Aaron home run record," said Mom. "Here, set the table while I finish making the salad. And speaking of home run records, how are you doing on your capitals?" she asked.

"Okay. Mrs. Dow gave me a makeup test today. I missed the first test because of my concussion."

"A test? You didn't tell us there was a test," said Mom. "You just said you have to learn them. How did you do?"

"I got about half."

"Eliza Daly!"

"That's not so bad."

"That's terrible. If we had known there was a test today, we would have reviewed them all with you last night."

"I worked on them with Panda every night."

"Clearly that wasn't enough."

"Mom, we have this test every year. Some of the other kids didn't do as well as I did."

"I don't care about the other kids. If you were expected to learn the capitals for a test, you should have learned them."

"I did my best."

"Eliza, you're a very smart girl," said Mom. "If you had done your best, you would have gotten all the capitals right."

Eliza looked at the milk glass in her hands. She remembered a scene from her mother's friend's Jewish wedding where the groom had smashed a glass under his foot. Sometimes in Greece, her father said, they threw glasses at the wall. Eliza did not smash the glass under her foot, and she did not throw it against the wall. Carefully, she put the glass down by her place at the table. Then she took a deep breath and turned to her mother.

"Look, Mom. I'm ten years old. I'm in the fifth grade. I did better on the capitals this year than I did last year. Next year, I'll be eleven. I'll be in the sixth grade, and I'll remember more capitals. Even the teachers don't expect us to learn everything at once. You told me not to expect Panda to learn how to sit and shake hands at the same time. First she has to learn how to sit. Then she learns how to shake hands."

Mom and Dad looked at each other. Dad cleared his throat. Eliza knew she had scored a hit. Maybe a home run.

"All right, Eliza," he said. "We don't expect you to be perfect. But we do expect you to tell us more about what you're supposed to be doing at school. And you can start right now, because you're not going to the Tail Waggers Club dog-obedience classes unless you get your work done."

"I have to write a report on Queen Elizabeth I."

"How long a report? When is it due?"

"It's due in three weeks. It has to be at least three pages long, but it can be longer if we want. It has to be neat, because we're going to bind them for display on parents' night. That's the night we have this year's Evolution Unit play, and I have to be an amoeba. I did forget to tell you that, but I just found out yesterday."

"I wish they'd let you do the same creature every year. That kangaroo costume was hard to make, not to mention the pterodactyl," said Mom.

"The point is to learn about different creatures, Mom."

"Well, we'll discuss the Evolution Unit costume later. What have you done about Queen Elizabeth so far?"

"I've read a really boring article in the encyclopedia, and I have to go to the public library for a biography because the one in the school library doesn't have any pictures."

"Why do you have to have pictures?"

"Otherwise I don't know what she looks like, or Henry VIII, or any of his wives, or Bloody Mary, or Edward VI, or the Earl of Essex, or—"

"All right, Eliza, you've made your point," said Dad. "We'll go to the public library tonight, right after dinner. I think I've got some pictures in my English history books too. One of the most famous portraits of Elizabeth actually has a name. It's called *Mirror of Grace and Majesty Divine.*"

"No kidding. Wow, what a terrific title! That's what I'll call my report, Dad: 'Mirror of Grace and Majesty Divine.'"

The words sang like music from the tape player. Mirror of Grace and Majesty Divine, Mirror of Grace and Majesty Divine. What a great name for a rock video. Eliza could see it now. Why didn't the dumb encyclopedia talk about Mirror of Grace and Majesty Divine? Even Panda liked the sound of it. She cocked her ears and tipped her head to one side while Eliza sang "Mirror of Grace and Majesty Divine" until the words bounced off the kitchen wall.

"Cut it out, Eliza," said Dad. "Let's eat dinner and get going before the library closes. You can have an extra half hour to read in bed tonight if you want."

Any excuse to stay up later than usual put Eliza in a good mood. The librarian found a book with lots of pictures, and Eliza read about Queen Elizabeth for a half hour that night and a half hour the next day in Sustained Silent Reading. She planned a Queen Elizabeth costume for Halloween, and she even read about Queen Elizabeth over the weekend because she and Susie weren't playing together.

"Where's Susie?" asked Mom on Saturday afternoon. "She's usually camped out in your bedroom by now."

"We had a fight."

"You were fighting in school?"

"It was a phone fight."

"About what?"

"Fleas."

"Was this something personal, or just fleas in general?"

"Personal. She left a message on the answering machine

that Sweetpea has fleas and Panda gave them to her."

"Most dogs have fleas at one time or another. The solution is a flea collar, not fighting with your friend."

"Well, you can tell her that. She started it."

"Why don't you stop it?"

"I already left a message on her machine to go scratch herself."

"Come on, Eliza; you're ten years old now. Not everything's black and white, remember? Even Queen Elizabeth had to compromise, remember? It may be Susie's fault, but you're not always an easy person to be friends with."

"I never get any practice, Mom. Mary never comes home. Susie lives in a lakeshore high-rise. The kids on the block are always doing something after school—and then they go to summer camp, which you and Dad won't send me to because you believe in family vacations."

"That's one reason I wanted you to stay in after-school sports."

"All we did in ASS was play ball. I didn't even know everybody's name."

"Eliza, I'm not going to argue. All these things may be true, but arguing still makes you hard to get along with. It's a problem. Call up Susie and tell her to come on over and watch that TV special this afternoon."

Eliza could feel her own eyes beginning to roll. "That TV special is pretty boring, Mom. It's one of those films with clay people that oomph around saying 'Hey, hey, what a beautiful day.' We could watch MTV instead."

"Actually, it is a beautiful day out, and you need some exercise now that you're not in after-school sports. Why don't you take Panda for a walk? You're certainly not going to watch MTV. And Eliza, put on your sunblock. The sun is blazing."

Fuss cuss. Eliza got up, stretched, and turned away, grumbling to herself. "First she fusses at me for not doing schoolwork. Then she tells me to stop." Her head pounded. Concussion headaches hung on like warts. "First TV, then no TV." Eliza moved her mouth like a TV weather reporter with the sound off. "First this, then that. First, last, and always sunblock."

"I can't hear you, Eliza. You're mumbling. What did you say?"

"Nothing, Mom." Eliza reached for the leash. Panda leaped from a day-long sulk. First she had brought the rope and laid it across Eliza's feet, but Eliza had paid no attention. Next she had dropped the ball on Eliza's toe and barked sharply, but Eliza had paid no attention. Then she had rested her chin heavily on Eliza's lap and stared and sighed and stared and sighed, but Eliza had paid no attention. Finally, she had rolled her eyes and moped. Now, at the sight of the leash, Panda began to run in circles and wag her tail wildly.

"Come on, Panda, wag your tail back and forth or up and down, but not both. You look confused."

Panda's feathery tail swirled from side to side. She never argued back.

"That's better. Now you look queenly. You look regal. You look royal. You're a Mirror of Grace and Majesty Divine."

After their walk, Eliza began taking notes for her report. Most of her father's books were too hard, but they had a few good portraits, and she could read bits here and there. The more Eliza found out about Queen Elizabeth I, the more she felt as if she knew her. Queen Elizabeth was not an easy person to be friends with, either, but she was smart and strong and she got what she wanted in a world that didn't want her to have it. No matter what happened to her, Queen Elizabeth never gave up, just like Eliza's wart. Eliza found that sometimes when she was thinking of something entirely different, Queen Elizabeth would walk into her head. She never knocked. She just appeared. Eliza might be throwing the ball for Panda in the park, and there stood Queen Elizabeth, admiring Panda, with the whole court behind her, video camera rolling.

Finally, Eliza began writing her report. She did not ask Dad for help. Everything he knew about Queen Elizabeth came from the outside, whereas Eliza knew what Queen Elizabeth felt like inside. They practically had the same birthday. Well, they had birthdays in the same month. Elizabeth was an early-September baby and Eliza was a late-September baby.

Eliza wondered what the weather was like when Elizabeth was born. Mom said that Eliza was born on a beautiful day, with the fall leaves turning red. She said that Eliza's face was red too. Eliza wondered if the leaves were turning when Elizabeth was born. It must have been sad not to have a mother to tell you whether the leaves were turning red when you were born. *Queen Elizabeth looked sadly out the window by herself wondering, every September 7— year after year after year after year after year after year after year after year after year after year after year after year after year after year after year after year—till she was seventy years old and died, what the weather was like when she was born.*

When the report was finished, Eliza took it to her father. He was sitting with Mom in the living room, and he read it out loud.

MIRROR OF GRACE AND MAJESTY DIVINE
by Eliza Daly

Queen Elizabeth I was born September 7, 1533. Her birth-stone was SAPPHIRE, the same as mine. She ruled the whole British Empire from 1558 to 1603, and it would make a GREAT TV SHOW. Lots of exciting things happened during Elizabeth's reign. Francis Drake sailed around the world — just like a NATIONAL GEOGRAPHIC SPECIAL. William Shakespeare wrote plays for the Globe Theatre. That might not sound exciting, but at the Globe Theatre everybody YELLED OUT LOUD when the plays got boring. It was pretty noisy.

Elizabeth's family life sounds like a SOAP OPERA. Her father, King Henry VIII, first married Catherine of Aragon. She gave birth to a baby girl, Mary, but Henry wanted boys. He had the marriage declared null (not dull) and void and married Anne Boleyn. They had Elizabeth — ANOTHER GIRL! After that, Henry divorced and beheaded Elizabeth's mother. Henry's third wife finally had a son, Edward, but then she died in childbirth. Henry divorced his fourth wife and executed his fifth wife. He acted like a MALE CHAUVINIST PIG, but he died before he could do anything to his sixth wife.

Meanwhile, Elizabeth always felt LEFT OUT. Edward got to be king when he was 10 years old, but he didn't last long — just 6 years. Then it was Mary's turn, which meant trouble for Elizabeth. Mary was NOT a wonderful sister. People called her

BLOODY MARY because if they didn't worship God as Catholics, they might be burned alive. Some of Mary's enemies got together and organized a rebellion in Elizabeth's name against Mary. Mary was so mad that she locked Elizabeth in the Tower of London for a while.

Finally, Mary fell ill and died, and Elizabeth became QUEEN at the age of 25 years (Nov. 17, 1558 — just 38 days before Christmas). After Elizabeth turned QUEEN people liked her, especially because she allowed them to worship God in any way, even though she kept an eye on the Catholics. Mary Stuart, Queen of Scots, was a Catholic who wanted to be queen of England herself. Elizabeth, being just like her father except not a male chauvinist pig, didn't fool around. First she had Mary Stuart locked up and later had her head cut off. When the executioner moved the body, he found Mary Stuart's little Skye terrier hiding in her skirts. It had followed her to the block and stayed loyal to the end. It refused food and died of grief.

Once Elizabeth almost died of smallpox. Today, she could have watched TV in the intensive care ward, but they didn't have such things then. She called upon a doctor, who said she had smallpox. Elizabeth was so angry at this that she turned the doctor away. Hot tempers ran in the Tudor family, but Elizabeth's temperature was hotter than her temper. The guards went to fetch the doctor again. He refused to come unless Elizabeth said she was sorry for turning him away. A guard swore he would kill the doctor if he didn't come, so the doctor cured her and tried to heal her pox marks. Elizabeth didn't let anything stop her, even when she had to COMPROMISE.

Many of her subjects called her GOOD QUEEN BESS because they thought she was so wonderful. However, being wonderful depends on your point of view. The Irish did not think she was wonderful, since she crushed them during the Irish campaigns. And even though she loved the Earl of Essex, she had him beheaded because he disobeyed her.

Elizabeth would never marry. Many of her council begged her to, but she knew that if she married, the king could rule the queen because in those days people thought women were too weak to rule and should have no power. Fortunately, we know better now, but it's still a fight sometimes. (For instance, how many U.S. presidents have been women?) Queen Elizabeth NEVER GAVE UP even when she felt all alone. She had no real family except England. Her father killed her mother when Elizabeth was little, then her father died, then her brother died, then her sister died, then her cousin was killed, and Elizabeth never had a husband or child. No one says whether she had a dog, but one painter showed a little spaniel at her feet. (Spaniels were called spaniels because they came from Spain.) Maybe after she got her spaniel, she wasn't so lonely anymore.

Elizabeth had many portraits made of herself, the most famous being MIRROR OF GRACE AND MAJESTY DIVINE. Sometimes she held an orb and scepter, or rode on a white warhorse and carried a flag with Tudor roses on it. She was well known for her beautiful eyes and slim fingers (no warts), but mostly for her STRONG WILL. She was the best queen ever before, and so far, after.

THE END

Dad put the papers down in his lap. "Eliza, this is a wonderful report. You've brought Queen Elizabeth right here into the room with us."

"I'm proud of you," said Mom. "It shows a lot of work."

"Was it okay that I said she was lonely? None of the books said that. I just made it up."

"You made a good guess based on facts," said Dad. "It shows a lot of empathy with your subject."

"I used to be lonely without Panda."

"I know that, Eliza," said Dad. "It's a good thing we got her."

"Well, I've been thinking, Dad. You know how we go to Ireland in the summer for vacations while you write about Irish history?"

"Yes, I know that."

"And how we're going again next summer and we have to leave Panda alone with some stranger who takes care of the house because we can't take her back to Ireland with us because of the quarantine?"

"I've thought of that."

"And how she has to stay alone all day while I'm at school and you're both at work?"

Mom looked at Eliza. "We know all that, Eliza. What's this leading up to?"

"Well, I was thinking. Maybe we should get another puppy to keep Panda company."

"Eliza, we just got this one."

"We've had her most of the summer and fall. I've taken good care of her, haven't I? I clean up her poop and take her for walks and feed her and everything. She hasn't had any accidents for a long time. All she did was chew up a few old shoes."

"And the newspaper."

"You had already read most of it, Mom."

"And a few Persian rugs."

"They were old too."

"They're supposed to be old, Eliza. They were antiques."

"Mom, you know how you always say people are more important than things? Well, animals are more important than things too. We could even save an animal from death at the dog pound."

"Honestly, Eliza, sometimes I feel as if we're living in a courtroom. Have you ever considered becoming a lawyer?"

"Mom, would you CONSIDER getting another puppy to keep Panda company? You don't have to decide now. It could be a Christmas present. Panda will settle down by December. She'll be a different dog when she's seven months old. Just like Humphrey. Christmas vacation would give us time to start training a puppy."

"Put it on your Christmas list, Eliza," Dad said with a sigh. "And why don't you find a folder for this report so it doesn't get chewed up?"

"I'm going to make one, Dad. I'm going to make one right now. I'm going to decorate some construction paper with circles and triangles and sapphires and Tudor roses and maybe a picture of the spaniel at Elizabeth's feet. Then I'm going to bind it like a book. Mrs. Dow showed us how. Hey, that rhymes. Mrs. Dow showed us how, Mrs. Dow showed us how, Mrs. Dow showed us how, Mrs. Dow showed us how. Come on Panda, let's go."

Eliza ran out of the room with Panda tangled in her legs. She could just imagine a spaniel puppy tumbling after them, romping around her room, curling up with Panda at night. She smiled at the little puppy sleeping in her head. Neither Mom nor Dad had said no. Step number one.

10. Dog in Disguise

Eliza turned around and around until her entire body was wrapped like a mummy in black telephone cord. "Okay, I'm sorry I told you to go scratch yourself. So what are you going to be for Halloween?"

"I don't know," said Susie.

"You could be a flea."

"That's not funny, Eliza. What are you going to be?"

"I'm going to be Queen Elizabeth, and Panda's going to be a spaniel."

"I can't think of anything to be except a witch or a fairy."

"You're always a witch or a fairy, Susie. Why don't you be Mary Stuart Queen of Scots, and Sweetpea could be your Skye terrier, and I could cut off your head while she hides under your skirt."

"Eliza!"

"Just kidding. How about if you're Mary Stuart Queen of Scots and Sweetpea is your Skye terrier and I DON'T cut off your head? We could trick-or-treat together then."

"What are you going to wear?"

"I'm wearing my bridesmaid dress from my aunt's wedding, with a crown which I'll make from cardboard and aluminum foil, and I'm going to tie long ears on Panda. You could use the dress Mom makes me wear to concerts."

"You told me that was really ugly."

"Well, it would be okay for Mary Stuart Queen of Scots."

"Thanks a lot, Eliza. Anyway, Sweetpea's ears are too long for a Skye terrier."

"You could fold them up with a clothespin, or wrap her head with a bandage and pin pointy cardboard ears on top."

"Eliza, I don't think I want to trick-or-treat with an ugly dress on and my dog's head wrapped in a bandage.

Why don't you be Mary Stuart Queen of Scots and wear the ugly dress, and I'll be Queen Elizabeth and wear your bridesmaid dress?"

"You can't. Your name's not even Elizabeth."

"So what? My name's not Mary Stuart, either. Besides, I can be Queen Elizabeth if I want to."

"No you can't. I thought of it first. All you can think of is witches and fairies."

"Eliza, that is totally and absolutely UNFAIR! I was a ghost once."

"Big deal. You wrapped up in a sheet and shouted 'boo' at everybody. And the sheet wasn't even white. It was PINK with flowers all over it. You looked like a TV ad for room deodorant."

"Eliza Daly, I don't know why anybody would want to trick-or-treat with you. I don't even know why anybody would want to be your friend."

Eliza looked at the phone. A dial tone hummed quietly in her hand. She was beginning to feel a terrible post-concussion headache coming on.

"Well, Panda, if that's how she feels, we'll just trick-or-treat all by ourselves. Some people have no imagination and no sense of humor. Some people are so dumb, they can't even carry on a telephone conversation. But you, Panda, are not one of them. You are going to love your long ears. Let's go cut them out right now. We'll sew them on that little headband I outgrew, and you'll look like a new dog."

Panda ran up the stairs and sniffed enthusiastically at the sewing basket as Eliza found the remains of a worn-out white flannel nightgown, cut it up with scissors, and assembled a set of long, fringed spaniel ears, which she sewed with large, uneven stitches onto her old headband. Panda stayed enthusiastic right up until the moment when Eliza leaned down and slipped the elastic headband over her perky black ears. Then she shook her head and backed away and tried to paw the spaniel ears off.

"No; bad dog. That's your Halloween costume, Panda. Stop it!"

One spaniel ear now hung over Panda's nose. She snapped at it and bucked backward as it flapped in front of her eyes. Finally she seized it between her sharp teeth, shook it back and forth, and fled down the stairs. In the living room, Eliza caught up with her, grabbed one of the spaniel ears, and tried to pull it away.

"Drop it!" she yelled.

Panda hung on and pulled. Her white teeth curved around a happy growl as she dug her feet into the rug. The elastic stretched. The stitches ripped. Eliza and Panda both fell backward with one ear each, Panda's hanging out of her mouth and Eliza's dangling from her hand. For a long time they sat and looked at each other.

Then Eliza folded her spaniel ear carefully and walked over to the downstairs phone and dialed Susie's number.

"Hi, Susie," she said softly into the phone. "One thing about Queen Elizabeth. She compromised when she had to. So I was thinking we could both be Queen Elizabeth."

"How can we both be Queen Elizabeth?"

"Well, we can take turns. For half the trick or treat you can be Queen Elizabeth and I'll be a spaniel. For the other half I'll be Queen Elizabeth and you can be the spaniel. Panda doesn't really want to be a spaniel at all."

"How are we going to get a spaniel costume?"

"I was a kangaroo in the Evolution Unit play last year, and we can use the furry body and change the tail and ears. I made some ears this afternoon."

"All right, Eliza. If you promise not to boss me around anymore, I'll come over next weekend and try it out."

"I don't boss you around."

"Promise."

"I don't boss you around, and I won't boss you around."

"Then I'll trick-or-treat with you."

Eliza said good-bye, hung up the phone, and walked slowly into the living room. Panda had buried her nose in the other spaniel ear and was watching to see if Eliza would play tug-of-war again. Eliza went back into the kitchen, got a dog biscuit, handed it to Panda, and quietly slipped the spaniel ear from under her paws while she munched on the dog biscuit. Then Eliza went to look for her old kangaroo costume.

She looked for the kangaroo costume all during the week. It was not hanging in the closet, or stuffed on top of the closet shelf, or trampled on the closet floor with all the shoes and boots. It was not in any of her dresser drawers, even the bottom one where she shoved all the dirty clothes that her mother made her pick up on cleaning day. It was not in the toy chest where she kept her dress-up stuff.

"Go find my kangaroo costume, Panda; go fetch it."

Panda raced wildly around the room and returned with a dirty rolled-up sock, which she dropped hopefully at Eliza's feet.

"No, that's not it, Panda. Nice try. Let's go ask Mom."

Mom was on the living room rug doing sit-ups.

"Twenty-five, twenty-six, twenty-seven—no—twenty-eight—I don't—twenty-nine—know where—thirty, thirty-one, thirty-two—it is—thirty-three—Eliza—thirty-four —but if—thirty-five—you kept—thirty-six—your room —thirty-seven—NEATER—thirty-eight—you wouldn't—

thirty-nine—have so much—forty—trouble—forty-one—finding—forty-two—the things—forty-three—you need—forty-four, forty-five, forty-six, forty-seven, forty-eight, forty-nine, fifty."

Neater, sweeter, beat her.

On Friday after school, Eliza divided her room into zones, like the ecology zones she had studied last year on a field trip to Prairie Park. Everyone in the class had all drawn straws, and Eliza's zone was the first twelve inches off the ground, which she did not want because it meant crawling around in the tall grass with bugs popping up in her face. However, it was a very successful twelve inches because she made a longer list of different plant and animal species than anybody else, including her assigned partner, dumb Joshua Houple, who was the only one left after dumb Laura grabbed Susie's hand and wouldn't let go. Since Stupid Houpid wouldn't cooperate over who was going to hold the magnifying glass, Eliza held it the whole time and found a lot of very tiny prairie life.

The kangaroo costume would not require a magnifying glass, but Eliza worked methodically. She started at the door of her room and crawled along investigating the twelve-inch zone above her floor. Crawling over the stuff on her floor seemed a lot harder than hopscotching over it. In fact, she felt more as if she were wading through deep water than crawling. *The flood waters rose higher and higher as Eliza waded through the house in search of Susie, who had been spending the night when the dam broke. Eliza had just volunteered to go downstairs for more popcorn, even though it was Susie's turn, when the waters poured into the first floor. Now with the lights out and the house in total darkness, Susie's cries for help seemed to echo off every wall. Eliza's intrepid search dog surged ahead as the water swirled in. Panda's paws thrashed and she struggled to swim with her nose pointing toward the terrified Susie.*

"Eliza, what are you doing on the floor?"

"I'm looking for my kangaroo costume, Mom."

"Well, you're not going to find it down there."

Eliza had just reached the bed and was peering underneath it to the far corners past a mound of gray dust balls and twisted pajama bottoms. There along the wall—just out of reach—stretched a long sturdy tail stuffed with cotton batting, thick where the kangaroo balanced for jumping and tapered to a point at the end.

"I found it!" shrieked Eliza. "I found my kangaroo costume!"

"What do you want it for, anyway?" asked Mom.

"Susie and I are going to take turns being Queen Elizabeth and a spaniel for Halloween."

Mom shook her head slowly and walked away while

Eliza carefully pulled the tail past the dust balls and shook out the furry costume attached to it. Perfect.

Taking the tail off was easy, even though it seemed a little like surgical amputation. *This won't hurt a bit, said the surgeon as she whipped out her scalpel.* Eliza made a new tail, spaniel-size, from the flannel nightgown and sewed on the spaniel ears she had rescued from Panda. Then she sewed up the opening Mom had made for a toy baby kangaroo to stick its head out. *From pouch to pooch in thirty minutes—a medical miracle!* Eliza had just slipped the costume on when the phone rang. She lifted up one long spaniel ear and put her head close to the phone.

"Hello?"

"Eliza?"

"Yeah, when are you coming over tomorrow? I just found the costume and made a new tail and ears. It looks great. I might even let you be Queen Elizabeth the whole time."

"Eliza, I can't come tomorrow."

"Why in the world not?"

"My mom found her dream house in the suburbs and she says we all have to go out and look at it."

"You're MOVING?"

"I don't think so. This is the fifth dream house she's found, and we haven't gone anywhere yet."

"Oh, so they're only looking around for fun."

"It's not much fun. We just walk from one room to another and hear all about the appliances."

"Well, I'll go ahead and work on the Queen Elizabeth costume, and we can try everything out next weekend. We still have plenty of time before Halloween."

On Saturday, Eliza snuck several pieces of cardboard from her father's starched dress shirts, taped them together in a circle, cut points to look like a crown, and wrapped the whole thing in aluminum foil. Then she pasted some flashy fake jewels from a necklace to each point of the crown. On Sunday, she made a papier-mâché orb for Queen Elizabeth to hold in one hand, and a foil-covered scepter made from the cardboard center of a roll of paper towels to wield in the other. "She'll have to carry her trick-or-treat bag on her head, Panda, but she'll be gorgeous."

"Eliza," called her mother. "Come down to the kitchen this minute."

Panda skittered down the stairs. Eliza turned away from the costumes draped over her bed and followed more slowly.

"What is this mess?"

Flour, water, and torn newspaper littered the floor. A huge wad of unrolled paper towels billowed on the countertop.

"I was making an orb and scepter for Susie's Queen Elizabeth costume."

"First of all, you know to clean up after a project. Second of all, why are you making Susie's costume?"

"I'm sorry I didn't clean up, Mom. I'll do it right now. And I'm working on Susie's costume because when we made up after our fight I promised she could be Queen Elizabeth if we trick-or-treated together, but she couldn't come over this weekend, so I wanted to get started on it. This is part of a compromise, Mom. You are the one who told me I should compromise."

"I didn't know it was going to involve redecorating the kitchen."

"Don't worry, Mom. Panda's already licking up the flour and water, and I'll pick up the newspaper and roll up the paper towels."

"All right, Eliza, get busy."

Eliza put on her favorite tape of the Strolling Tones, turned it up to top volume, and got out the mop. "You're pretty good at this, Panda, but there are a couple places you missed. Is your tongue tired? We did a good weekend's work. Susie's going to love it."

The next morning at school, Eliza described her progress on Queen Elizabeth and the spaniel. Susie was very quiet. On Tuesday, Wednesday, Thursday, and Friday,

Susie stayed quiet. After dinner Friday night, Eliza called her up.

"So when are you coming over to try on the costumes?"

"Eliza, my mother and father bought that house."

"Oh."

"They said they've been waiting forever for just the right one, and this is it, and it's ready for occupancy, and we're moving before Halloween because my father's been transferred to the suburbs."

The phone got very quiet. Then Eliza heard a wild yapping in the background as Sweetpea click-click-clicked over the wooden floors of Susie's fancy high-rise apartment.

"You're really leaving?"

"As soon as we can pack up."

"Do you think you'll come back for trick-or-treating?"

"Maybe," said Susie doubtfully. "It's a long way, and my mother says she never wants to set foot on that expressway again."

"Doesn't she drive her car on the expressway?"

"You know what I mean, Eliza."

"I know what you mean, Susie. I have to go now."

"Eliza, I'm sorry we can't trick-or-treat together. I really wanted to be Queen Elizabeth and her spaniel."

"Me too."

"I'll still be in school next week."

"I'll see you, then."

Eliza hung up the phone and looked at Panda, who followed her up the stairs while she stuck her bridesmaid dress back in the closet and set the crown, orb, and scepter on the shelf above it. Then Eliza put on the spaniel costume and curled up on her bed, where Panda jumped up and began to lick her face.

"I guess we'll both be dogs for Halloween," said Eliza, and she blotted her wet eyes with fringed flannel spaniel ears and rocked Panda in her arms. *The Halloween moon rose on two figures slipping through the shadows. A giant spaniel and a medium-small Border collie barked at every door, "Trick or treat, trick or treat, give us something good to eat." Their bags filled up with gumdrops, fudge, jelly beans, butterscotch, taffies, toffees, chocolate bars, popcorn balls, peanut clusters, caramel apples, and candy corn galore. Then they disappeared into the night for a forbidden feast, a long-drawn howl, and a wild run down the road, where the wind was a torrent of darkness among the gusty trees. . . .*

11. Dogfights

Eliza bounded up the stairs, with Panda crowding behind her, and hopscotched over three pencils, one box of Kleenex, and a tube of glue. Unfortunately, Panda tripped her, and Eliza stepped on the glue, which popped its cap and oozed coldly through her sock.

"Yuck! Gross, Panda. I'll be stuck to the floor forever." Eliza peeled off the sock and rubbed the glue from her foot with wads of Kleenex, which fell like gummy white flowers around her.

"You won't believe this, Panda, but Mary is coming home. Finally! You haven't even met Mary yet! That's because she's never home. Wonderful Mary works all the time. She has a job, plus she gets all A's at school. You will love Mary. Everybody does. But you will love me more, right? Don't ever forget, you are MY dog. Right?" Eliza nodded Panda's head up and down.

"AND, we—I—get four days off from school now. Let's HEAR a doggerel CHEER!

"Wednesday afternoon, all's well.

Four days off is a magic spell—

Thursday, Friday, Saturday, Sunday.

YEAH, THANKSGIVING HOLIDAY!"

The beautiful cheerleader leaped into the air while her sister slam-dunked a ball and the crowd cheered for them both. "They're wonderful girls," said their mother modestly, "each in her own way. Winning this Thanksgiving game has been a highlight for us all."

"This is your first Thanksgiving, Panda. Thank goodness the Pilgrims landed. Without the Pilgrims, we'd have to go from Columbus Day to Christmas without a break. Give thanks for Thanksgiving!" Eliza bowed Panda's head by pushing down gently on her pointy nose. Panda sneezed.

Mom appeared at the bedroom door and winced at the sight of the floor. "Hurry up, Eliza; Mary's plane is due in soon. There's a snowstorm on the way, and the traffic will be terrible."

"I'm hurrying. Can we bring Panda?"

"Certainly not, Eliza. The airport will be a zoo."

"That's great, Mom; she'll fit right in."

"Eliza, I'm counting. One, two, three . . ."

Eliza scurried to get her shoes on. She knew that at the count of ten, Mom would be out the door. Mom had no mercy on slow starters.

The traffic was terrible, the snow was thick, and the airport was a zoo. Fortunately, Mom and Mary were almost the same height, so they could see each other over the crowd. And everyone could hear Eliza shrieking at her sister.

"MARY! You grew your hair! HAIRY MARY!"

Everyone turned to stare at Mary's hair.

"Pipe down, Parrot Mouth. You sound like a megaphone. Hi, Mom." Mary gave Mom and Eliza a huge hug, both at the same time, which squished Eliza against Mom's and Mary's bosoms. Eliza did not have a bosom yet, and personally, she didn't miss it. She ducked out from under Mary's arm and circled around them. Mom and Mary stood there gushing for a few minutes and then, with their arms across each other's shoulders, slowly started toward the baggage-claim area. Eliza skipped backward so that she could watch them. They looked exactly alike.

"Turn around, Eliza; you're going to run into somebody," said Mary in her bossy voice.

"Don't be so slow, then," said Eliza. "You walk like a sick turtle."

"Girls, don't start," said Mom.

Eliza turned her back on both of them. "Yak yak, Mary's back," she said softly.

Suddenly Mary swooped down on her from behind and tickled her armpits. Eliza screeched and tried to run, but Mary held her fast. "Don't pout, Fuss Face," she said. "I have a surprise for you in my bag."

"What is it?"

"If I told you—" said Mary.

"—it wouldn't be a surprise," finished Eliza.

"You have to wait till we get home."

"When we get home, you get a surprise too. You get to see Panda."

"Now it's not a surprise, Dodo."

"Panda is always a surprise."

"Mom told me about Panda. Lucky you. Mom never let me have a dog."

"Really?" asked Eliza. "How come?"

"Because I'm not as strong-willed as you are, that's why."

Wow, strong-willed Eliza. Just like Queen Elizabeth. Eliza made her way strongly through the crowd and strong-armed Mary's bag into the car while Mom and Mary chattered away behind her. Eliza was the queen of the family, the leader of the pack. After loading the bag into the back end of the car, she pranced around to her place beside Mom in the front seat. Mary was sitting in it.

"Hey, Mary, no fair. That's my place."

"Too late, Eliza; I got here first."

"Mom."

"Don't make a fuss, Eliza. Your sister just got home."

Eliza made a gorilla face at the back of Mary's head and a fish face at the back of Mom's. Naturally, they paid no attention to her. But when they all got home, Panda went crazy over Eliza, wagging her tail like a snowstorm and acting as if Eliza had been away for months. Mary, on the other hand, got a polite sniff from Panda and one little wag and that was all. Ha!

Dad had fixed an early dinner so that he could start working on the Thanksgiving feast for Thursday. Mom had to coach a night game. For once, Mary didn't sit around yakking but volunteered instead to go with Eliza to the snowy park, since Panda had missed her afternoon walk. Before they left, Mary rummaged around in her suitcase and produced the surprise, a racquetball racket that she'd bought secondhand so that Eliza could hit a ball across the park for Panda.

"Whoopee! She'll be the best-exercised dog in the world!" yelled Eliza as she rolled a tennis ball around on the racket. Panda stared at the green ball as if it were a sheep about to run away from its flock. In the park, she did a flat-out run after the ball, which arched into the air when Eliza whacked it and almost disappeared from sight into some bushes.

"This is great, Mary. My arm gets so tired throwing that ball," said Eliza.

Panda bounded back over the snow and dropped the ball in front of Eliza's feet.

"She's really good at that," said Mary.

"The best," said Eliza. "Nobody's as devoted to tennis balls as Panda."

"Well, maybe Billie Jean King in her prime," said Mary.

"Not even Billie Jean King," said Eliza. She kept hitting the ball and Panda kept chasing the ball and the snow kept falling and Mary kept stomping her feet to keep warm.

Mary was the first to give up. "It's time to go home, Eliza."

"One more ball," begged Eliza.

"Just one," said Mary. "It's really getting dark."

Eliza said:

> The wind was a torrent of darkness
> among the gusty trees,
> The moon was a ghostly galleon tossed
> upon cloudy seas. . . .

Mary said, "That poem used to spook me."

"Me too, till I got Panda. She likes 'The Highwayman.' I say it to her at night."

"She doesn't know poetry from poppycock."

"She does. Panda's a very intelligent dog. She knows three state capitals already."

"Dream on, Baby Sister."

Eliza hit the ball as hard as she could, and it sailed into the night with Panda sailing after it. This time, Panda did not come back. They waited.

"Panda!" yelled Eliza.

"Here, Panda!" yelled Mary.

The snow fell without a sound.

Both girls ran across the park toward the bushes where Panda had disappeared. There, by the light of a streetlamp, they could see that Panda had dropped to her on-guard position. She was watching the ball, but the ball was in the mouth of another dog—a half-grown, raggedy brown dog with long ears and a shivering body so thin that its backbone stuck out.

"Oh, look," said Eliza. "The poor thing, it's shaking. And look at its ears. Maybe it's a spaniel."

"It looks more like a caterpillar crossed with a basset hound. Its ears are longer than its legs!"

"They are not. It's a beautiful dog."

"Eliza, that's the funniest-looking dog I've ever seen."

"Well, you'd be funny-looking if you were that cold and hungry."

"I'm pretty cold."

"You're pretty funny-looking, too, Mary."

"Cut it out, Sprout," said Mary.

"This dog will freeze to death out here," said Eliza. "We have to take it home."

"Mom will have a fit," said Mary.

"We'll keep it in the basement," said Eliza. "Just for tonight. Then we'll put up signs."

"What if nobody claims it?"

"Panda needs company."

"Good luck, Eliza. You're going to need it."

Eliza slowly approached the dog and held out her hand. Except for its shivering, the dog did not move. When Eliza got close, it dropped the ball at her feet and sat down.

"Look at that, Mary, how well-behaved it is. I bet this dog is already house-trained!"

"Fat chance," said Mary. "Does it have a collar?"

"Nope." Eliza slipped the leash out of her coat pocket and looped it around the dog's neck. After one tug, it trotted behind her obediently. Panda picked up the ball and followed, while Mary jogged past her.

"You're never going to get that dog in the house, Eliza," shouted Mary over her shoulder.

"We'll see," said Eliza.

Thanksgiving dinner was delicious. The mashed potatoes looked like a big, white, fluffy cloud against the blue sky of the plate. This was probably as close to flying as the turkey would ever come, thought Eliza as she watched the sunny butter melt. Someday she would be a vegetarian. She pointed the slice of turkey toward the cloud and arranged the beans below to look like green grass. Two spears of broccoli made trees, with cranberry sauce flowers around them. Eliza herself had helped make the pumpkin pie, which looked like mud but tasted like sugar, spice, and everything nice—everything little girls were supposed to be made of, said the nursery rhyme. Personally, Eliza preferred snakes and snails and puppy dogs' tails, but Mom said both recipes were sexist. "Little girls are made of blood, sweat, bones, and tears, just like little boys," said Mom. "Don't let Hollywood fool you."

Eliza looked up to see Mom staring at her. Everyone else seemed to be staring at her too.

"Eliza, I asked you a question. What are you going to do about that dog? I didn't have the heart to turn it out in the storm last night, but you have to either find the owner or call the humane society."

"The humane society won't be open today, Mom. It's Thanksgiving. Besides, the humane society is not very humane. They kill dogs after forty-eight hours if no one shows up to claim them."

"Well, we can't keep it in the basement forever."

"It's a she, Mom, not an it. And females are calmer, you know. I was thinking we could bring her upstairs today. When I checked this morning, she hadn't made any messes, and she followed Panda everywhere when I took her out. In fact, she seems to love Panda."

"How does Panda feel about her?" asked Dad.

"Panda's thinking about it. You know how lonely Panda gets while I'm at school."

"Eliza, dogs don't think. They either get along or they don't," said Mary.

"Well, Panda hasn't bitten her yet."

"That's a start," said Dad.

"They just sort of growl at each other and play dogfight."

"Like you and Mary," said Dad.

"Right, Dad, and you wouldn't put Mary in the dog pound. So can we keep her while I put up signs, Mom, and not call the humane society?"

"Keep Mary or keep the dog?" asked Dad.

"Keep both," said Eliza. She looked over at Mary with pleading eyes. "Mary thinks we should keep her too; right, Mary?"

Mary rolled her eyes—just like Mom did—and said nothing.

Mom sighed and rubbed her forehead. She did not roll her eyes. "I suppose so, Eliza, but don't think this is going to be a permanent arrangement. Right after you and Mary do the dishes, I want you to start putting up signs around the neighborhood."

"Oh, Mom, you've just saved a life. I'll do the dishes every night forever."

"You have to do the dishes every night, anyway, Potato Head," said Mary.

Eliza glared at her. "I'll do them without fussing, then, Carrot Nose."

"Get on with it, girls," said Dad. "Your mother and I are going to take our coffee into the living room."

When they were gone, Eliza started scraping and rinsing the plates for the dishwasher. "Thanks a lot for helping me keep the dog," she said to Mary sarcastically.

"I'm not going to be here to help take care of it. Mom's the one who will end up doing all the work."

"That's not true, Mary. I take care of Panda all by myself. You think I'm still a baby, but I'm not. You're never around to see how much I do."

Surrounded by crystal glasses and serving dishes and pots and pans piled all over the kitchen, Mary filled the sink full of hot water, squirted in the detergent, and swished it around.

"Plus, I'm old enough to wash the dishes now," said Eliza. "You can dry, Neat Freak." Eliza pushed Mary aside and plunged her hands into the water.

"Mess Pest."

"Clean Bean."

"All right, Banana Breath, so you're growing up."

"Thanks, Beet Brain." Eliza spattered her soapy fingers at Mary's shirt.

"Don't break anything, or I'll report you to the humane society." Mary cracked her towel against Eliza's backside. "I missed you, Egg Eyes."

"I missed you, too, Corn Ears," said Eliza.

"So how are you going to find this dog's owner?"

"I'll put up signs this afternoon and ask around at the park."

"Eliza, that dog's too thin to have gotten lost yesterday. I think she's been straying for a while. You're going to have to find a new home for her."

"I know that. I was thinking maybe we should groom her and name her and feed her for a little while so she'll look healthier. That way, somebody will be more likely to give her a home."

"What are you going to name her?"

"Muttface."

"Oh, that will attract a LOT of prospective owners!"

Eliza smiled. The fewer prospective owners, the better. When Mary left Sunday, there would be a new family member to take her place. An even trade—Muttface for Mary. Eliza washed the last dish, dried her hands, and opened the basement door.

12. Doggedly Determined

Mary did not come home for Christmas because of her college job. Eliza opened presents with no one to tease her and played with them all by herself.

On December 31, Eliza watched the ten o'clock news intently, along with her parents.

Behind the reporter, dogs barked and whined in rows and rows and rows of cages. The reporter stretched out his hand as one puppy thrust its nose through the wire and cried for attention. Then he turned back to the viewers, while the frantic sounds faded till his voice could be heard again. "And so we conclude the last of our post-holiday special reports on animal abuse. As the new year begins, let's all remember to have a heart for nonhumans, too."

Dad clicked the TV off. He and Mom and Eliza sat together on the couch staring at Panda, who waited patiently beside her tennis ball for the next commercial. Panda wagged her tail. Then she began to look guilty. Finally she turned her head away. It made Panda nervous to be stared at.

"How can anybody just abandon a dog?" demanded Eliza. "To wander around alone and starve, or get hit by a car? People should be sent to jail for that."

"Maybe serving time in an animal shelter would be more to the point," said Dad.

"You know, your sister did her senior report on animal abuse," said Mom. "She was mainly interested in horses, but she did a lot of general background reading. Maybe you could ask her about it the next time she calls."

"Maybe."

"Or maybe you'd like to do your own report," said Dad.

"What I'd like to do is smash all animal abusers to smithereens."

"Hot-tempered Queen Eliza."

"No, really, Dad."

"Well, realistically, how would you go about changing things?"

"I don't know. It's hard being a kid. Nobody really listens to you."

"Oh, I wouldn't say THAT, Eliza," said Mom. "You can be pretty effective. Just look at your dogs."

Everybody looked at Eliza's dogs. In front of the TV set, Panda ducked her head between her paws. Over by the Christmas tree, which Eliza would not let her parents take down until school started again, slept Muttface. Muttface was no longer thin and funny-looking. She was now plump and funny-looking.

Eliza took a deep breath.

"Three dogs probably wouldn't be much more trouble than two. And you know how everybody says charity starts at home? You say that yourself, Dad."

Mom rolled her eyes.

"Mom, please don't roll your eyes before I finish."

"I think you've already finished, Eliza. We've heard this before."

"No, you haven't. Before, I wanted a dog because I was lonely. Then I wanted a dog so Panda wouldn't be lonely. Now I want a dog so the dog won't be lonely. There's a big difference."

"There is a big difference, Eliza, but if you start watching the news regularly, we could end up adopting the whole world. There are a lot of lonely babies out there."

"Well, Dad, that's an idea. If you don't want another dog, we could adopt a baby instead. Since Mary's in college now, I could have her room, and somebody else could take mine. I'd make a wonderful sister."

"You're already a wonderful sister, Eliza."

"OLDER sister. We need a baby. Mary had me, but I don't have anybody."

"You have Panda!"

"That's true, but now Panda has Muttface, and that leaves me out again. If we adopted a baby, then Panda and Muttface and the baby and I would never be lonely. Plus, we'd be doing something besides sitting around talking in front of the TV. You know how Dad always says put your money where your mouth is. And you know how you say we're all part of the world's problems. This way, we could be part of the world's solutions. And Mom, maybe the baby would grow up to like ASS."

"Eliza, it's time for bed."

Eliza kissed Mom and Dad good night and turned to go.

"Tell us, Eliza Daly, what led you to become head of the world's largest orphanage?"

"I always dreamed of being a big sister, but my parents would never adopt a baby—even though, as I often told them, I was

desperately *lonely. So I decided when I grew up to take care of all the babies no one would adopt."*

"How do you support all these babies?"

"We appeal to the public through news broadcasts. It's important for all citizens to get involved with what's going on and help solve the world's problems."

"And how do you keep all these babies happy?"

"Dogs. Dogs are the secret. We take in a lot of homeless dogs, which the babies love, and which love the babies, so no one's ever lonely. It's a wonderful *sister system."*

As Panda followed Eliza to the stairs, Muttface woke up and tumbled after them. Muttface clearly thought Panda was wonderful, but Panda wasn't used to being a big sister yet and paid no attention to Muttface. Getting used to being a big sister must require time. Eliza stopped at the door of Mary's room. Maybe she'd sleep in Mary's bed tonight, just to get used to it. Maybe if she begged a million years, using steps one through one thousand, her parents really would adopt a baby. Eliza definitely deserved a turn at being biggest and best.

A cold nose, thin and pointy, nudged her left hand for attention. Another cold nose, large and snuffly, nudged her right hand for attention.

On second thought, maybe she'd try some baby-sitting first. It was great to have a sister around sometimes.

It was also great not to have a sister around sometimes. A baby would be around all the time, like a wart. Warts required a lot of patience.

Eliza walked into Mary's room, which was perfectly neat.

"If I have to be neat to be a big sister, forget it," Eliza said to the adorable adopted baby in Mom's arms.

"Hey, are you pushing this big-sister deal for me or for yourself?" asked the adorable adopted baby.

"I'll think about that," said Eliza.

Both dogs trotted after her to the bathroom and stared adoringly while she brushed her teeth. Both dogs followed as she went into her own room and hopscotched across three chewed-up sneakers, one glue-stiffened sock, several gummy white flowers of Kleenex, yesterday's underpants, and her report on Queen Elizabeth, marked with a big red A. Both dogs jumped on the bed after Eliza, Panda on one side of her and Muttface on the other. Both dogs pricked up their ears when Mom suddenly screeched with laughter downstairs. Dad could always make Mom laugh, no matter how gloomy she got.

Sweet dreams, Mom; sweet dreams, Dad; sweet dreams, Panda; sweet dreams, Muttface; sweet dreams, Mary; sweet dreams, adorable adopted baby . . . maybe . . . someday.

As Eliza settled down, Panda politely stayed by her

feet, but Muttface crawled slowly, inch by inch, toward her chest and curled as close as possible with a soft whine. Eliza threw her arm around Muttface's furry fat stomach and mumbled, "Good dog. I'll come to thee by moonlight, Muttface; that's what the highwayman says to his bonny sweetheart Bess. 'I'll come to thee by moonlight, though hell should bar the way.' And I will, Muttface, so don't be lonely. You have me. And I have you. And you have Panda, and I have Panda. And you have Mom and Dad, and I have Mom and Dad. And sometimes, when Mary's home, we have Mary. And in our hearts, truly and forever, we're all together."

Downstairs, Mom and Dad laughed. Panda sighed. Muttface snored. Eliza slept.